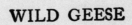

WILD GEESE

WILD GEESE

BY

MARTHA OSTENSO

GROSSET & DUNLAP
PUBLISHERS   NEW YORK

PRINTED IN U. S. A.

To

MY FATHER

WILD GEESE

CHAPTER I

1

IT was not openly spoken of, but the family was waiting for Caleb Gare. Even Lind Archer, the new school teacher, who had come late that afternoon all the way from Yellow Post with the Indian mail carrier and must therefore be hungry, was waiting. Amelia Gare, Caleb's wife, with all her cheerful bustling about the kitchen as if everything weren't quite ready, could not break the suspense. Judith and Charlie had milked several of the cows, and had come in and out of the house repeatedly for no reason whatever. Martin, slow and clumsy of feeling as he was, had cleaned the entire stable so thoroughly that it looked unnatural. Ellen, Martin's twin, was playing the organ, but appeared to have forgotten even the more familiar parts of her repertoire, such as *Red Wing* and the less recent *Ben Bolt*. Ellen played, harmoniously enough, "by ear."

The Teacher sat quietly in the low red plush rocker, listening to the springs of it exclaim as she rocked to and fro. She reflected, with some misgivings, on the noncommittal opinions that had been expressed at Yellow Post the day before in reply to her delicately asked questions about the Gares. She remembered also, with increasing dis-

comfort, the short, scornful grunt of John Tobacco, the
mail carrier, when she had sought from him what manner
of being she might expect in Caleb Gare. Now, the
squeaking rocker kept her mind off her hunger. The
rocker seemed to say, "Caleb! Caleb! Caleb!" It
amused the Teacher, rather wanly.

Presently the outer door swung open. Judith had come
in again. Lind Archer saw her against the dim light of
the lantern that hung by the kitchen door. She had a
great, defiant body, her chest high and broad as a boy's;
her hair was wild-locked and black and shone on top of
her head with a bluish luster; her eyes were in sullen
repose now, long and narrow; her lips were rich and
drooped at the corners. She wore overalls and a heavy
sweater, and stood squarely on her feet, as if prepared
to take or give a blow.

Judith approached Lind with a heavy, swinging stride.
Lind thought she had never before seen such vigorous
beauty.

"Are you hungry?" the girl asked her abruptly.

"A little," Lind admitted.

Ellen's hands paused in mid-air over the organ keys.
Her eyes held a reproach as she looked at Judith. But
the younger girl, ignoring her sister, took a few long steps
and disappeared into the pantry. She emerged with a
plate on which were two slices of bread well-buttered, and
a glass of milk.

Ellen's reproach grew. She stood up before the organ.
"Jude, you know father doesn't——"

"This won't spoil your supper any—if you're ever goin'
to get it," said Jude to the Teacher, breaking in upon

Ellen's speech. Lind took the proffered food, too embarrassed to refuse it.

Ellen rose erectly and without a word walked into the kitchen. Lind felt that she was conferring in a whisper with her mother. The Teacher nibbled uncomfortably at her bread and took a sip of the milk.

Jude, who had been winding a bit of twine about a stick, threw herself on the floor at Lind's feet.

"You might as well know that he'll try to bully you," she said matter-of-factly. "He's starting by keeping supper waiting. He always does the same thing when a new teacher comes. He expects you to be a man. All the teachers have been men. He's in for a jolt. But you stick up for yourself, Miss Archer. Don't you let him bully you."

Amelia spoke from the doorway.

"Judith!"

"Never mind, Ma. I'm only tellin' her the truth."

Ellen came back into the room and placed a pitcher of water heavily on the table, as if she had miscalculated the distance between the table and her hand. A pucker of anxiety drew her brows together. Ellen wore silver rimmed glasses that were not originally prescribed for her. As a result the pupils of her eyes were always dilated and strained, the lids reddish and moist. She stood before the table for a moment and shot a bitter glance in the direction of Judith. Then she passed quickly out of the room.

Lind Archer finished her bread and butter in silence. There was a raw feeling in the air that no superficial remark could dispel.

Judith, apparently bent on tormenting her sister Ellen, whistled to her dog where he lay in the niche under the staircase. The dog looked up.

"Caleb!" she said sharply. The dog started, pricking up his ears.

Jude smiled maliciously toward Ellen, who moved about the kitchen as though she had not heard.

"You see—" said Judith, then began on another line. "He loves to ride around in the cart to show the Icelanders how much spare time he has during the busy season, while the rest of us slave around in the muck all day."

A feeling of apprehension was growing upon Lind. The high romance which had attended her setting out for this isolated spot in the north country was woefully deserting her. She had never before looked upon the naked image of hate. Here it was, in the eyes of a seventeen-year-old girl.

The light, gritting sound of wheels came from outside. Ellen returned to the organ stool, her face, for all its youth, bearing the hard serenity of a strong woman in a crisis. Lind wondered why the occasion should call for such fortitude.

"Judith, you had better call Martin," Ellen said in a thin voice. "Father has come."

Judith got to her feet without a word.

In the kitchen, Amelia hastily cleared the sink and placed in it a clean basin of hot water. She whipped the towel from its roller and put a fresh one in its place. Untying her apron, she straightened her dress and combed her hair briskly back before the cracked mirror on the wall.

Then the door opened. At first, Caleb seemed to be a huge man. As he drew into the center of the kitchen, Lind could see that he was, if anything, below medium height, but that his tremendous shoulders and massive head, which loomed forward from the rest of his body like a rough projection of rock from the edge of a cliff, gave him a towering appearance. When attention was directed to the lower half of his body, he seemed visibly to dwindle. He had harsh gray hair that hung in pointed locks about his head, a weedy, tobacco-stained mustache, and startling black brows that straggled together across the bridge of a heavy, bony nose. His eyes were little beads of light that sought Lind out where she sat in the lamp glow of the other room. He did not speak until he had hung his coat and hat on a peg, and had washed himself at the sink.

Lind saw that with Caleb was a frowsy-looking farmer in a red mackinaw. He also relieved himself of his outer garments and sat down without a word on a chair in the kitchen. Mrs Gare spoke to him but he answered only in broken monosyllables which Lind could not distinguish. The Teacher noticed, however, that Amelia addressed him with the same calm deference that had been in her attitude when Lind first met her in the barnyard that afternoon, upon her arrival with John Tobacco.

Caleb did not speak until he had finished washing. He did not so much as touch a comb to his ragged hair.

"Skuli will stay the night," he announced finally to Amelia. His voice surprised Lind. It was remarkably soft, almost like a purr.

"But I have no extra bed. The teacher has come," Mrs Gare protested mildly.

"The teacher—yes, of course—the teacher. Skuli stays the night," he repeated, with no more emphasis in his voice than when he had first spoken.

He called Skuli and proceeded, with a sort of hulking shuffle into the dining room, which constituted the other part of the ground floor of the log house, and also served as a living room.

"You are the teacher, I suppose," he said, seating himself near the iron stove with his back half turned from Lind. There was nothing in the expression of his face to indicate that he was surprised to find the new teacher a girl. She rose and extended her hand, which he ignored. Lind flushed helplessly.

"This is the other trustee of your school, Skuli Erickson," said Caleb, with an elaborate sweep of his hand toward the Icelander.

Lind gave Skuli her hand and he shook it heavily.

"There should by rights be three of us," Caleb went on in a wearied tone, as though he was giving perfunctory and tiresome information that might as well be dispensed with, "but there ain't been another appointed since old Josh Curtis died. Out here in this unorganized territory things go on much as the weather sees fit. And I don't know but what it ain't just as good with the two of us. Eh, Skuli?"

Skuli uttered a grunt which might have been an affirmation or a denial. He was slightly deaf, spoke very little English and understood little more.

In a few minutes they were all seated for supper, Lind between Ellen and Martin, Skuli directly at the other end of the long table from Caleb Gare.

"Looks like an early spring, eh, Skuli?" Caleb called to the Icelander.

Skuli nodded. "Ya," he agreed, helping himself well to potatoes and gravy.

There was a silence, during which the food was passed around the table. The children, all except Judith, sat with their eyes lowered to their plates, shame-facedly self-conscious in the unused presence of one so pretty and dainty as the new Teacher.

"Much rain down your way lately?" Caleb asked Skuli, calling the length of the table. Amelia glanced with faint dismay from her husband to Lind.

"Naat muts," Skuli replied. "Soom last veek. Purty dry."

Throughout the meal Caleb exchanged observations with the brief-spoken Skuli. You would have thought Skuli the honored guest of the evening. Lind looked across at Jude, whose eyes were smoldering. The Teacher smiled. Caleb's evident obliviousness of her was not half so humiliating to her as it was to Judith.

After supper the situation remained unchanged. Caleb ignored the Teacher as cleanly as if she were air. She withdrew to the horsehair couch in a corner and opened a book. Martin and Charlie, the youngest of the family, went out to finish milking, while Judith scraped and piled the dishes and removed them to the kitchen.

"Play us a piece, Ellen, play us a piece," Caleb requested. He and Skuli had drawn their chairs up to the stove in the center of the room and had taken out their pipes. A feeler of blue smoke curled up and around Caleb's head. Lind was reminded of a painting she had once seen of the fixed, sardonic face of a fakir, lifting his eyes upward to catch the demoniacal image of his conjuring.

While Judith helped in the kitchen, Ellen obediently went to the organ. She sat erect and prim in her washed-out gingham dress, that had apparently shrunk and grown too small even for her narrow shoulders and uncertain breast. Her fine brown hair, that was lighter in color and much less luxuriant than Judith's, was drawn back without a relenting wave from her rather prominent, austerely white brow. Her eyebrows were exquisitely shaped and black as ink-lines. Behind the magnifying glass of her spectacles her dark blue eyes swam liquid and vague. Her raw-looking, thin fingers sought out the keys.

"Yes, Bjarnasson's got the best fishing sites, no doubt about it—no doubt about it," Caleb declared in a loud voice, while Ellen played *Lead, Kindly Light*. "But he'd better not get to thinkin' he's goin' to hog the whole lake. Not by a damned sight—not by a damned sight. I'm goin' to send Martin over there one of these days with some new nets—too far to do anything during the freeze-up. What do you think about it, Erickson? Is he showin' you any fight?"

"Na-aow," Skuli grunted. "He geev me v'at I vant, de dirty djevil. I tak it first."

Caleb and Skuli both broke into stormy laughter at the Icelander's joke. Ellen faltered over the keys. Caleb glanced sharply at her and she hurriedly picked up the thread of the song. Judith came in from the kitchen and sat down on a fur rug on the floor. Her dog followed and snuggled his head in her lap. The girl sighed and leaned wearily against the wall. Lind noted again how strangely beautiful she was. Like some fabled animal—a centauress, perhaps.

Caleb launched upon an account of an involved sale of timber, at times almost shouting into Skuli's ear to make clear to him the technicalities. The strains of the hymn mourned lamely to an end. Ellen hastened into a patriotic march, stumbled over the keys, shifted to a lullaby and then to a waltz. A spot of red showed on either cheekbone. Her mouth was tightly drawn, her chin flat and long so that in profile she looked like an old, tired woman.

Amelia came and stood by the table. She turned up the wick of the lamp slightly. As she did so, the light picked out the shadows under her eyes, the rigid lines about her mouth, the pale sandy hair whitening about her temples. Amelia was fifty and was beginning to put on flesh, but she bore herself with a dignified reserve that seemed almost a part of her physical being, so that the grace which was hers in youth still clung to her. She seemed preposterously ill-fitted to her environment. Lind was filled with pity as she watched her move about the room, picking up a paper, straightening a doily, or, from a habit Lind realized must have been formed in another life, pulling down the shades before the windows. Amelia must surely have been worthy of a better lot.

"That reminds me," Caleb Gare began again. "How did you make out with those furs you sent to the Siding? Grini buy 'em up?"

"Ya-a. Gode monney." Skuli said, sucking comfortably at his pipe. "Fur-rrs—naow gode. Grini, he's fool himself. Hee! Hee!"

"Did I show you that wolf pelt Martin got east of here? Big beast he was too, eh, Martin? Where's the pelt? Find the pelt, Martin. Made a rug out of it, Skuli—you ought to do that with some of yours. Here —Jude—show Skuli the rug!"

Martin had crossed the floor to take the rug from Jude. The girl got up slowly. Her resentment flooded in a dark wave across her face.

"Skuli has seen it three times already," she muttered, snatching up the rug. Martin took it from her, a half grin on his face at her anger. Martin had long since learned the futility of indignation. He was twenty, past.

Caleb smiled blandly.

"Skuli forgets what a rug it is. Heh, heh!" His laugh was genial.

The Icelander examined it again, to please his host. He commented upon its quality, then handed it back to Caleb, who sat holding it while he resumed his talk.

Judith called Pete, the dog, and strode out of the room.

Amelia sighed and sat down with a lapful of worn stockings and a handleless cup over which to mend them.

Presently Judith returned, without the dog, and seated herself beside Lind. Caleb still held the rug.

Charlie was playing solitaire at the table.

"Here, Charlie," Caleb said to him. "Bought ye a new deck of cards at Yellow Post to-day. Couldn't think of anything to buy the girls—they have everything."

Judith thrust her shoes out before her. The toe-cap was off one of them. Amelia glanced at her quickly and shook her head in protest behind Caleb's back.

Ellen yawned behind her hand.

"Cheer up, Ellen my dear, we'll all be goin' to bed soon," Caleb said. "Skuli and I are both tired. Had a hard day, eh, Skuli?"

Judith sprang up.

"Well, I'm goin' anyway!" she asserted.

Caleb looked gently at Amelia, pointing with his pipe at Jude.

"Mother, Jude had better be lookin' to her manners, eh?" he suggested in his softest voice.

Amelia's eyes darted to Judith.

"Judie—remember——"

The girl reseated herself carelessly enough beside Lind, but the Teacher saw that her hands were clenched. Lind felt then that, like the other members of the household, she would come to hate and fear Caleb Gare.

2

It was so arranged that Judith slept with Lind that night. Amelia begged the Teacher to overlook the irregularity—Skuli, the Icelander, must be accommodated

The great loft was curtained off into three compart-
ments—the bed rooms of all the children and such infre-
quent guests as chanced to come. In the room below
Caleb and Amelia slept; their bed was a cabinet during
the day, folded up against the wall.

The floor of the loft was composed of pine boards
scrubbed white and smooth. You could look down
through a knothole and see the stove glowing red in the
darkness of the room below. Above, the rough, cobweb-
hung rafters leaned down upon you; and on a wild night a
jet of wind would ripple over your cheek if you lay with
your face to the wall. In a winter dawn even tiny sift-
ings of snow might be found in the crease of your pillow.

Judith undressed. When she came to her undergar-
ments she put her nightgown on with her arms free beneath it, so that she might finish disrobing in this manner.

She watched Lind taking off her trim outer clothing.
When she saw that she wore dainty silk underthings she
glanced at her more covertly. She made no comment.

After both girls had undressed, Judith picked up a
string of amber beads Lind had placed on the stand
near the bed. There was also a pair of ear rings of the
same limpid yellow substance.

"Wild honey! Drops of wild honey!" Judith exclaimed in a whisper. "Just the color of you!"

Lind looked at her curiously. "You may have the
beads, Judith," she said on an impulse.

Judith laughed. It was a rich laugh, from her deep
young lungs. "My, wouldn't I look funny with them on!
Specially, cleaning the stables. No, thanks. They were
made for you, Miss Archer."

When the girl was asleep beside her, Lind, restless in her new surroundings, knelt at her window and looked out into the night. There was still a pale glow from the sunset, and the land stretched out black and remote under it.

3

Far out across the prairie a lantern was swinging low along the earth, and dimly visible was the squat, top-heavy form of a man. It was Caleb Gare. He walked like a man leaning forward against a strong wind. He frequently went out alone so, with a lantern; no one knew where, nor why; no one asked. Judith had once told Amelia scornfully that it was to assure himself that his land was still all there. . . .

Caleb pressed on through the half-dark, leaning forward as if against some invisible obstacle. Presently he came to a ridge from which he could look east and west, north and south, upon the land that was his; the two tame hayfields, separated from each other by a neck of timber belonging to Fusi Aronson (it would be well to own that timber, a fine stand it was); the dark, newly plowed furrows where in another five months the oats would again be stirring like a tawny sea under the sun; the acres where barley and rye would be sown for cattle feed, vanishing into the blue night toward the south; the small rectangle of wheat that he raised for chicken feed; the acres of narrow woodland stretching northward like a dark mane upon the earth; and the good, flat grazing land with two bluffs, that might have extended farther westward had it not encountered the holdings of that miser, Thorvald Thorvaldson; and, beyond the muskeg and a dried lake-bottom, his cherished field of flax.

Southeast, under the ridge, bottomless and foul, lay the muskeg, the sore to Caleb's eye. In the heat of summer it gave up sickly vapors in which clouds of mosquitoes rose. Cattle and horses, breaking through the pasture fence and heading for the hayfield, had disappeared beneath its spongy surface. South of it lay his flax field, the most precious part of all his land. To get rid of the useless land and buy in its place the neck of timber held by Fusi Aronson: that was an honest ambition and one to be achieved. That Fusi Aronson would part with his right hand rather than sell him a square inch of ground, Caleb knew all too well. But many a better man had been glad to part with a right hand in certain exigencies. There was the little matter of Bjorn Aronson's slight dishonesty, for instance, that was not generally known in the community—that little discrepancy in Bjorn's moral balance that hurt Fusi more than any other thing on earth. What a comfort it was to Fusi that Bjorn was now one of the trustees of the Yellow Post church fund, a connection that would surely brace his manhood and beat into him a true metal. Caleb smiled as he thought of the trusting Fusi. Something might come up that could be used to good advantage. Somehow he would use brother against brother . . . he would wait.

Caleb felt a glow of satisfaction as he stood there on the ridge peering out over his land until the last light had gone. He could hold all this, and more—add to it

year after year—add to his herd of pure bred Holsteins
and his drove of horses—raise more sheep—experiment
with turkey and goose for the winter markets in the
south—all this as long as he held the whip-hand over
Amelia. Amelia's word would start the children, then it
would be all over—the results of his labor would be swept
from these fields like chaff from a barn floor. He was too
old to carry on alone. Hired help was worse than none—
lazy, treacherous, rapacious. As long as he kept track
of the outcome of that little folly of hers. . . . And,
so far, he had managed very well. True, he might at any
time lose that little contact—the boy, good Lord, he must
be a man now—might even die. He had come out of the
war safely, in spite of Amelia's praying . . . oh, no
doubt the woman had prayed that he would die! But
it was an uncertain world. Amelia, she was a soft fool,
thank God! Not many women would be so conveniently
sentimental and self-sacrificing for the sake of a son born
out of wedlock—and that son a man grown, and a
stranger to his own mother. Well, if she was loth to
have Mark Jordan learn of his parentage, Caleb Gare
would not reveal it to him—providing that Amelia kept
her place and did not force him to. . . . Mark Jordan
was a fine young fellow, too, according to Bart Nugent.
Bart had kept track of him very well, in the town where
Caleb was unable to do his own spying. The good fathers
in the mission had taken Amelia's story for truth, and
Mark had grown up with the solid idea that he was the
last of a family of saints. There was a joke for you!

The war had saved the boy from the priesthood, Bart
Nugent had thought, and it had also radically altered his

philosophy. He had always been interested in architec-
ture, and had gone into it seriously after the war. Bart
had written that a nervous disorder had lately developed
in Mark Jordan from over-work, and that he might take
to farming for a spell. Perhaps—the coincidence was
not beyond thought. . . . It might not be well, however. . . . Amelia might weaken if she saw him. There
was no guessing what a woman's reactions might be.
Amelia had loved the boy's father, that he knew. The
knowledge had eaten bitterly into his being when he was a
younger man and had sought to possess Amelia in a manner different from the way in which he possessed her now.
In that earlier passion of the blood he had found himself
eternally frustrated. The man who had been gored to
death by a bull on his own farm in the distant south had
taken Amelia's soul with him, and had unwittingly left
her bearing in her body the weapon which Caleb now so
adroitly used against her. His control over her, being
one of the brain only, although it achieved his ends, also
at moments galled him with the reminder that the spirit
of her had ever eluded him.

Caleb lifted the lantern and examined the wick.
Things would turn out to his liking. He would hold the
whip hand. Judith, yes, she was a problem. She had
some of his own will, and she hated the soil . . . was beginning to think she was meant for other things . . .
getting high notions, was Judith. She would have to
be broken. She owed him something . . . owed the
soil something. The twins, they would stay—no fear of
their deserting. Martin and Ellen would not dare to
leave; there was no other place for them. And Ame-

lia, she was easy . . . yes, yes, she was easy, Amelia was!

Caleb glanced again at the coveted bit of woodland, and crossed the ridge toward home. After he had crawled through the barbed wire fence that surrounded the second hayfield he turned down the wick and blew out the flame in the lantern. No need of wasting oil. . . .

4.

Lind woke to the comfortable drowsiness of farmhouse lofts and piece quilts, and the inarticulate outdoor sounds of early spring mornings. Something had wakened her. She did not know then that it was the three knocks of the broom handle upon the ceiling of the room below, which was nothing else but the planks of the loft floor.

She lifted herself upon her elbow and looked down upon the dusky rose cheek of the girl beside her. Judith was more than three years younger than Lind, but somehow there was a wisdom that Lind did not share in the bountiful, relaxed beauty of her body as she lay asleep. An intangible fragrance rose from her, like warmth. Like the warmth of milk, or newly mown hay. Lind touched her lightly to waken her. Jude's eyes slowly opened, veiled like a waking child's. She yawned and stretched her round, strong arms above her head. Then she turned over on her stomach and lay for a few moments without speaking. Lind got out of bed and prepared to wash.

"I hate to get up," Jude declared from the pillows. "Some day I'm going to have a silk bed and lie in it for-

ever, and hear cows bellowing right at my elbow and know
I don't have to get up to water 'em.'"

Lind laughed at the absurd picture, while she saw the
pathos in it. Three more knocks sounded peremptorily
against the floor, and the Teacher turned questioningly
toward Jude.

Judith drew herself lazily out of bed and began to pull
on her stockings under her nightgown.

"You'd better hurry," she said to Lind. "There goes
Ellen down."

Lind wrinkled her brows. "You don't mean that *I*
must hurry?"

"He won't let breakfast be kept for anybody," Jude
told her briefly.

Lind was thoroughly amazed. "But it must be only
five o'clock! Whatever shall I do every morning until
nine?" she exclaimed.

"Hm-p!" Jude retorted, relishing the perverse contempt she felt for the Teacher together with her admi-
ration and envy. "You might milk a cow or two, or chase
skunks. There's lots of 'em in the bush. That's Pete
after one now. Hear him barkin'? The smell ain't bad
—*isn't* bad—when you get used to it."

The Teacher shook herself free from the annoyance she
felt at Caleb's rigor, and resolved to make the best of
it. After all, it was rather amusing.

Breakfast, it turned out, was a meal eaten in almost
complete silence. It was a fixed duty discharged without
zest. Except Jude, the children did not seem half awake.
The toil of the day before hung about them still like a
tedious dream.

"Guess we'll plow up that fallow field over east, after all, Martin," Caleb said, settling back in his chair while he wiped his mustache with his hand. "Jude can start it all right this morning, eh, Martin?"

Martin continued eating his porridge. He was a slow eater, as he was a thinker. He could not quite appraise the meaning of his father's words. It was folly to seed the worn-out east field this spring. And as for Jude's plowing it—it was a heavy field, full of stones, difficult enough for a man. And hadn't there been talk of Jude continuing morning school as she had done last year, so that she might write her entrance examinations?

"Well—" Martin began solemnly. His face reddened as he found himself unable to protest. "Guess I could do it. Kind o' tough for Jude."

"Tough for Jude? Pshaw! Hear that, Jude? He says you can't do it! Guess there ain't a field that 'd stump you, eh, Jude? Some girl, that, Miss Archer. Look at the arm on her! Bigger'n mine. Heh! Heh!"

It was the first time he had addressed Lind that morning. The Teacher shrank from the tyranny so thinly veiled behind his jocularity. She ventured to smile at Judith, who appeared not to have heard her father's sally.

After breakfast, Judith went out to milk, and Lind accompanied her. The cow pen was overhung at one end by weeping willows, which were putting forth tiny buds. Judith led her cow to that extremity of the pen.

"It's a little prettier over here," she explained.

The cattle sheds and the shelters for the other animals were all of gray logs, the low roofs sodded and showing

faintly green now, although it was still cold and raw.
The ruts of the cow pen, since there had been no rain or
snow for weeks, were hard as cement, and reminded
Lind of the relief maps children made at school. The
deep tracks of the cattle were almost indistinguishable
from the human tracks intermingled with them. The
cold of winter had fixed them there and only the rains of
spring would wash them away.

"When did you stop school, Judie?" Lind asked. She
had seated herself on a stone near the girl, and was
watching the straight white stream of milk striking the
bottom of the pail with a thin churring sound. The
cow's flanks were satiny, her tail clotted with manure.
The animal looked over her shoulder with a round, vague
inquiry, and went on chewing her cud.

"Went half a day last year—every morning. Guess I
won't go at all this year. He hasn't said, lately. He
talked some about it during the freeze-up, and it sort of
cheered me up then. But I guess he didn't mean anything by it."

Lind felt her indignation mounting once more against
Caleb. This was criminal, denying the girl what education was at hand.

"Oh, my dear, hasn't your mother a thing to say about
it? Do you *want* to go?"

"Wantin' and goin' is two different things," she replied, looking into the pail between her knees.

"But Judith," Lind said earnestly, bending toward
her, "is there no way to arrange for your going—can
he not do without you here?"

"He *can,* but he won't. There's no use talkin'." Judith shifted her great body on the milk stool. She seemed to have grown suddenly shy, with this talk that lay so close to her inmost desires.

Lind rose and touched Jude's shoulder. As she did so Caleb appeared from the end of the barn. He glanced sharply toward the girls once, then looked studiously away.

"You'd best go. He ain't likin' you being here," said Judith.

Feeling helplessly a culprit, Lind picked her way back across the rutted ground. She decided to go early to the school house and air the place thoroughly before the children came. It would give her something to do.

5

There stood the school house, across the trail from the Gare farm. It was low and square, and built of uneven logs: the white paint of it had peeled and fallen off here and there in large flakes. There it stood, in unashamed relief against the gray green haze of spruce and tamarac.

Lind would have liked Judith's company that first day at school. A teacher who had formerly taught at Oeland had told her of how he had actually been trampled in a stampede that had broken out among the young ruffians from beyond Latt's Slough.

By nine o'clock, the school room, the porch outside, and the playground were over-run by the sturdy demons who had gathered from miles around for what was an acknowledged holiday. Lind rose from her desk and

rang a small bell, which instantly brought order out
of chaos.   There was a general scamper indoors, and
a hurried selection of the best and most remote seats by
the stronger of the small band.   Lind looked down upon
the children, and saw that every seat was occupied; a
condition that would never prevail again throughout the
term.   The children, some of them six feet tall and well
on in their 'teens, had come from every direction, even
from other districts—half of them with the sole purpose
of conveying to their elders their impressions of the
Teacher of Oeland, and with no intention of coming a
second day.

Lind sat at her desk and introduced herself.   There
was dead quiet while she spoke.   Every eye was fixed
upon her face.

"We are going to have a very nice time together here,
I know," said Lind.   "You will keep the seats you have
for to-day, and to-morrow I shall move you about according to your grades.   Don't you think that will be best?"
She smiled down at two of the ruddy cheeked girls who
sat together at one desk, and because their opinion was
thus sought, they nodded their heads energetically, and
afterwards whispered to each other how pretty the new
teacher was.

Lind opened a large black record book and began to
take their names, up one row and down another.

"Thorvaldson—Sophia, Anna, Una," Lind repeated
after three little girls in the foreground with pigtails as
white as snow.   Behind them sat two boys from Yellow
Post, half-Cree, who did not know their last names and

looked back in great fright to their elder brother who sat in the rear.

And so on down the line. The Sandbos, who lived two miles to the east of the Gares, and five of whom attended school. The black-eyed Hungarian Klovacz children, whose father had a homestead several miles east of the Sandbos. The Bjarnassons, who came from the great lake on the west, and drove seven miles to school. Swarthy faced young tartars from north of Latt's Slough, momentarily impressed and suppressed, most of whom were too old to go to school and would probably not appear on the second day at all.

Lind saw with relief that she had captivated the children. There would be no trouble. She looked around at the dingy whitewashed walls.

"We shall have to have some pictures," she said. "How would you like to do a little painting this morning?"

There was vigorous assent. A little apple-cheeked Icelandic boy from the Narrows and a half-breed girl from Yellow Post importantly passed around the paint boxes and the coarse paper Lind had found in the store closet.

And so the first day of school began at Oeland.

6

It was April and the little buds were opening stickily on the elms, and tingeing their boughs with purple and brown. The cottonwoods were festooned with ragged catkins. A softness was unfurling like silk ribbons in the pale air, and the earth was breaking into tiny warm rifts from which stole a new green.

The children came to school in the mornings with their arms loaded with the long green catkins of the gray birch, which Lind told them was the *Betula Lutea;* which they promptly forgot. The ditches along the wood road became a gray blur of pussy willows; and one day Lind heard the first robin. It was a time of intense wonder in the north, after the long, harsh months when the heart is shut out from communion with the earth.

Lind frequently walked alone through the green filter of light in the woods that led away from the Gare farm northward to the acres of Fusi Aronson.

She thought of Caleb Gare and Amelia, and wondered how a human soul could keep from breaking utterly. Lind had wakened early one morning and had looked out from her window to see Amelia staring with trans- fixed eyes at the dawn—at something beyond the dawn, it seemed. It was not like a farm woman to do that. There must be some reason for Amelia's endurance. Was it a hope of compensation of some kind? The children? No, there was not enough affection among them—after the precious flame had been sucked into the very earth upon which and by which they lived—to make the sacrifice worth while. There must be something else. . . .

On a Friday evening, Lind prepared to leave for the Sandbos', whose homestead was in sight down the wood road from the Gares'. Caleb and Martin were repair- ing the chicken house, removing the winter sod from the roof and sparingly inserting shingles wherever there was a leak.

Judith came out of the house with the Teacher, who had with her a small bundle. Mrs Sandbo would expect her to stay the night, at least.

"I'm going to ride down with you—the cattle are down that way," said Judith, glancing toward the chicken house, where Martin was standing on a ladder swinging a hammer upon the damp shingles. Judith turned toward the log barn that crouched like an old moss-backed turtle between the wagon-shed and the granary.

Except for the blows of Martin's hammer on the soggy shingles there was not a sound abroad. The air and the earth seemed to be held together in a glass bowl. There was that thin luster over everything that comes only on a clear April evening. The dank, clinging smell of newly turned soil rose like a presence.

Lind was glad that Judith was to accompany her. They would have many things to talk about. Even at her age, Judith had a certain fineness of mind which came to an extent, perhaps, from the seasonal contact with the teachers of Oeland, but more from a deep native consciousness drawn from Amelia. Lind delighted in the rich spontaneity of the girl, in her naïve reactions. She saw much less of her than she might wish to. Caleb saw to it that Judith was busy about the place or in the fields during the day, and at night she wished for sleep more than for the comfort of friendship.

The Teacher stood below Martin and talked to him while she waited for Judith. Caleb had gone into the tool shed near the barn.

"Martin, it must be wonderful to make things—and mend them, with your hands," she ventured. Martin talked so little. He had not yet voluntarily addressed her.

He looked down at her and half grinned, drawing in his under lip bashfully.

" 'Tain't so wonderful—got to do it in any kind o' weather," he managed to say. His long, dull face became suffused; he intently inspected another shingle.

Poor Martin! At twenty he understood only one thing: work.

Caleb came out of the shed. With his left hand he brushed the right side of his weedy mustache: a gesture that had become familiar to Lind. He did not look at the Teacher. She was rather glad that he had adopted the policy of ignoring her. It gave her more opportunity to watch him.

Judith, mounted on the mare, Lady, beckoned to Lind. Caleb turned and saw her.

"Too early to go for the cattle," he said, lifting the bank of his eyebrows toward her meaningly. "That old seeder has to be fetched from Thorvaldsons'. Charlie can bring in the cattle."

"Charlie can get the seeder," Judith said in a clear voice. She sat straight and formidable in her saddle, facing Caleb coldly. Of the two, Lind felt that the girl was the more to be feared, for sheer physical power.

"Did you hear what I said, Jude?" Caleb asked, handing a box of nails up to Martin. His voice was gentle, casual.

In answer, Judith wheeled the mare toward the gate

and started down the wood road. Lind mounted the pony that the Sandbo children had left for her. On the road she met Jude, her face dark with anger.

"I'm through putting up with it!" Jude flared. "He's got to quit thinkin' we're animals he can drive around."

They rode along together for a short distance. Then Judith turned to go back.

"It's no use—he'll take it out on Ma. He knows I'm goin' to the Sandbos'. Find out if Sven is really comin' home, will you, Lind?"

The Teacher had asked her to call her Lind.

She nodded in response to the girl's request and rode on down the shimmering wood trail. In the shallow ravine on either side lay a mist of flowering dogwood trees. Behind her, growing fainter now, came the thudding sound of Martin's hammer on the rotten shingles of the chicken house.

7

The Sandbos boasted a frame house, and a wire fence around their buildings, not a sagging wooden one such as the Gares did with. The entire place was so overgrown with chokecherry and wild plum trees that in a short time now the house and barn and cowshed would be hidden in a white nebula. This beauty was more by accident than by design, for Mrs Sandbo would have preferred the frame house to be in full view to passers-by the whole year round. Frame houses were rare at this distance from the Siding of Nykerk.

In a remote time, which Mrs Sandbo liked to speak of

as a year or two ago, the family had lived in a small
village where a locomotive and passenger coaches were
seen three times a week and where a freight train was a
daily sight and nothing to be marveled at. The Gare
children, never having been beyond a radius of ten miles
from home (save perhaps Martin and Ellen on their
trips with the cattle to Nykerk), had never seen one of
these wonders of modern times, and as for having ridden
in one—! Well, the Sandbos, all of them except little
Lars, who was born at Oeland, *had* ridden on the rail-
way. So, although they were friendly enough from Mrs
Sandbo's point of view, there was a gulf between the two
families that could not be spanned.

Mrs Sandbo, having lived in a village, awaited Lind in
the parlor. Emma, a ponderous girl of fifteen who still
attended school half days, was stiff and sober in a clean
dress which had been donned for the occasion.
She ushered Lind into the presence of her mother without
a word. She suffered, in fact, the sensation of strangling
until the Teacher was out of her sight behind the parlor
door.

All the blinds, except one, were closely drawn in the
room where Mrs Sandbo sat. There was a dry smell
of wall paper, as if the windows had been nailed down
since the day the room was decorated. Mrs Sandbo herself looked like wall paper, as if she had no sizable depth
but a crisp, flat surface, the back of which would be
gritty. On each of the four walls of the room, in geo-
metrically precise relation, hung an enlarged photograph
of one or more of the Sandbo family. The photographs
bore the rainy-day look of all enlargements. That

which first met the eye was an enormous likeness of the late Ludvig Sandbo himself, Mrs Sandbo's husband.

Lind entered and greeted Mrs Sandbo in her warm manner. Her hostess had been sitting on an upright set-tee of pale brown imitation leather and elaborately carved and scrolled oak.

"I em glad to see you, Mees Archer," Mrs Sandbo beamed with a square, Norwegian intonation. "Seet down. I vill get coffee. The girls say you like it at Gares. Iss that so? You are the first then, much so I hate to say it. But vait—the coffee cooks." She rustled out of the room without waiting for a word from Lind.

The Teacher sat down before the frame of Ludvig Sandbo. He had eyes like black shoe buttons. They chilled Lind. She moved to a chair near the lighted window.

Mrs Sandbo returned with steaming coffee and little round pink-frosted cakes.

She assailed Lind at once with questions, not so much to get an answer as to reveal to the Teacher her famili-arity with objects of the world beyond Oeland.

"Oh, yess, my husband, Ludvig, he vass there, many, many times," she interrupted when Lind mentioned the city she had come from. "It iss him, up on the vall. And a stinker he vass, too. .Good land, I say, t'ousand times a day, I em heppy he iss gone. Vhat he could drink, that von! Never vonce sober in six years!" She smacked her lips over her coffee cup and wiped her eyes with the corner of her apron.

"Was he not kind to you?" Lind asked gently.

"Kind? Him? Good land, I vass a dog under him. Now I live good, not much money, but no dirt from him, t'ank God!" She lifted her eyes up to the photograph, and Lind saw unmistakably a look of wistfulness in them.

"Hess Mrs Gare in her new teet' yet?" she asked presently, her pale eyebrows lifting eagerly above her glasses.

"I don't believe she has," said Lind, hesitating. "I think she expects to get them."

"Expects?" Mrs Sandbo almost snorted. "Her? She don't expect not'ing—not from *him*. She been getting these teet' now four five years while I get these two sets, and vhat have I got to buy vit' teet'? Old Gare— he got money to buy teet' for hundred head cattle. My man, he vass a devil, but he vass easy vit the money. He say, long before my teet' vass all gone, he say, 'Sigri, you tak couple dollar and go to dentist.' He vass alvays easy—*for* easy, I told him. Much for easy!" She looked fondly up at the photograph and sighed. This time there was certainly no doubt as to the wistfulness.

Lind was impressed. Mrs Sandbo hitched her chair more closely to Lind's and puckered her brows. She lowered her voice.

"Tell me—how goes it there? Iss he crenky vit you, too?"

"No, he hasn't bothered me," Lind told her.

"He's a rascal, Caleb Gare," Mrs Sandbo lamented with a shake of her head. "I feel sorry for the poor woman. To be married to such a man!"

"Why does she stand it?"

"Vell—" Mrs Sandbo hesitated mysteriously, "I vould not say it again, but they say who knows it, that he bragged vonce to von of the Icelanders that he hess it *on* her. Vhat more, I can not say. Vhat *you* t'ink, Mees Archer? She iss scared purty near cresy of him, I t'ink."

Lind could venture no opinion. Mrs Sandbo drifted into other subjects, then rose ceremoniously to show Lind about the place and to offer her the freedom of the entire farm.

Lind liked the Sandbos. There had been ten of them, but there were only eight left at home. They were big-boned children, solemn and hard working. The eldest daughter, Dora, had married and lived on a homestead north of Latt's Slough. Sven, of whom Mrs Sandbo spoke proudly, had gone to work in town. He was expected home in May.

Emma, the eldest daughter at home, spent much time thinking. At least her eyes were always downcast, her full, healthy face inscrutable. Lind watched her come up the path leading Rosabelle, the Jersey. She clumped along, a great hulk of a girl, in step with the cow.

"What are you dreaming about, Emma dear?" Lind called to her from where she sat on the stone step of the milk shed.

Emma looked up, confused.

Lind drew her down beside her on the step.

"What are you thinking of, Emma?" she asked again.

But Emma blushed more furiously than ever, and Lind concluded that if she had really been thinking of anything, it was just as well left unsaid. Emma kept her silence and got up to milk Rosabelle. Her thoughts were, indeed, too profound for utterance.

When Lind was out of sight, Emma burst into tears of emotion. The Teacher was too beautiful and too sweet. She could not endure familiarity with her.

Such was the effect of Lind's coming to Oeland.

8

On Saturday evening, Lind walked home through a fine mist drifting down from the swamps that lay to the northward.

Against the strange pearly distance she saw the giant figure of a man beside a horse. As she walked across the field he came toward her, and she saw that it was Fusi Aronson, the great Icelander. Lind had spoken to him only once before, when she and Jude had found the cattle over on his land.

He doffed his hat when she spoke to him, and returned her greeting in the quaint English that seemed odd in a man of his size. There was a vast, rough charm about the man. He was grand in his demeanor, and somehow lonely, as a towering mountain is lonely, or as a solitary oak on the prairie.

Fusi walked back with her along the margin of a stand of spruce that pointed up blackly above the mist.

"I was just thinking how lucky you people are up here to have spring so close to you," Lind said, glancing up at him.

"Yes, we are very, very lucky," he responded slowly, carefully. "But few of us know it."

"Don't you think most of the farmers realize it—in one way or other?"

"No," he said. "Here the spirit feels only what the land can bring to the mouth. In the spring we know only that there is coming a winter. There is too much of selfishness here—like everywhere."

His voice was deep, sonorous, the tone almost oracular, as if his statement were made as much to the air as to Lind. She looked at him furtively.

"I wondered just what Caleb Gare was feeling about this—this mist," she ventured.

"Caleb Gare—he does not feel. I shall kill him one day. But even that he will not feel." There was no anger in Fusi's voice. Only deep, prescient certainty.

Lind started.

"Why?" she murmured.

"He took the lives of two of my brothers. There was epidemic here with the Indians some years back. It was a snowstorm and my brothers asked in at his door. They were blind from the storm. They were not sick —my brothers. But Caleb Gare feared the sickness—it was the devil sickness—he feared for himself. And he closed the door in their faces. One I found dead a mile from Caleb Gare's farm, two day after the storm. He was frozen so stiff we could not put on him his Sunday clothes and he was buried just so he was. The other died from the cold. I could not get the cold out of him, how long I worked. But first he told me about Caleb Gare."

There was iron in Fusi's voice. His face against the

darkening air was like iron.   Lind was silent.   Fear had
come to her.   Fear of this harsh land.

Far overhead sounded a voluminous prolonged cry,
like a great trumpet call.   Wild geese flying still farther
north, to a region beyond human warmth . . . beyond
even human isolation. . . .

CHAPTER II

1

L<small>IND</small> stayed in the school house working over the children's lessons usually until the light faded and she knew the Gares would be sitting down to supper. Although they were crowded with work, these were lonely hours, when the last sunlight streamed in across the deserted desks and blurred with a vague gold the dusty blackboards, so that you could not make out the awkward figures that had been written upon them.

Lind would often take out from her desk drawer the letters she had received from home in the twice-weekly mail, and, ashamed and impatient with herself as she would feel afterwards, she could not check the tears that rose to her eyes. And then, strangely enough, she would wipe her eyes and suddenly realize that it was not herself that she had been thinking of at all, but the Gares—Amelia, with her inviolable reserve and quiet graciousness, behind which she lived who knew what life; Ellen, prim to a point of agony; Martin, the stumbling dreamer, forever silent in his dream; the boy, Charlie, whom Caleb pampered and played against the others; Judith, vivid and terrible, who seemed the embryonic ecstasy of all life; and Caleb, who could not be characterized in the terms of human virtue or human vice—a spiritual counterpart of the land, as harsh, as demanding, as tyrannical as the very soil from which he drew his existence.

The Teacher was lonely, and even more conscious of the stark loneliness of Amelia, of Judith, of Ellen and Martin, each within himself. Work did not destroy the loneliness; work was only a fog in which they moved so that they might not see the loneliness of each other.

Days came when the loam was black and rich with rain. Judith and Martin, being the strongest of the workers under Caleb Gare, carried the soil's heaviest burden. Judith mounted the seeder and wove like a great dumb shuttle back and forth, up and down, across the rough tapestry of the land. In the adjacent field Martin worked with the bowed, unquestioning resignation of an old unfruitful man. Occasionally Judith threw a glance at him. Then she would scowl and exclaim profanely to the plodding horse.

What with the work in the fields and the occasional trips with ax and saw into the bush there was not much time for play. And in the evening the body and the brain would be heavy with sleep, and there was nothing to do but throw one's self down like a spent animal, and seek oblivion from thought and feeling.

Lind felt that the rigid routine of the farm was imposed by Caleb to keep anything out of the ordinary from happening. And nothing happened; nothing happened. Day in and day out, not a soul came to the Gare farm; not a soul left it, not even to visit the Sandbos, two miles or less away. And Caleb went about with the fixed, unreadable face of an old satyr, superficially indifferent to what went on, unconscious of those about him; underneath, holding taut the reins of power, alert, jealous of every gesture in the life within which he moved and governed.

2

Sunday formed a sort of interval. Caleb was the only one of the family who attended church at Yellow Post, but since the minister preached there only every third Sunday, coming all the way from the Nykerk parish, the amount of spiritual guidance the others missed was not so great as it might have been.

It happened that the second Sunday after Lind's coming was Easter Sunday, and a new minister was expected to hold services. Amelia rose as early as on week days, although usually an hour's grace was allowed on Sunday, to prepare Caleb's breakfast and lay out his white collar and black broadcloth suit with the greenish velvet lapels. His shoulders were not so square as they had been the decade or so before when the suit had been bought, and the back of the coat hunched up and made a little groove just below the collar, which Amelia could not remove with any amount of pressing. Each time he put the coat on, she was afraid he would notice it and complain of her careless treatment of it. Amelia had had to wash the stiff collar he had bought through the mail order catalogue, and its wings had lost some of their contour in the starching. So that by the time Caleb rose and knocked on the ceiling to waken the children, and then came into the kitchen to wash, Amelia was thoroughly worried about how the day would go.

"Martin washed the gig over yesterday—after work. It looks real nice," she said to him cheerfully as he spread the shaving soap over his jaw. Ever since they were first married, Caleb had looked most human and likeable when he was lathering his face preparatory to shaving, and she had often approached him at such times with requests or confessions that she dared not make before or after his toilet had been completed.

Caleb stropped his razor blade to his satisfaction before he replied. He always took his time in answering Amelia. It gave him leisure to weigh his words and to create a certain uneasiness in the woman concerning his reply, that was flattering to him even when the matter under discussion was a trivial one. This morning he was in a generous mood.

"Martin did well. I'm half a mind to take him with me. He's a way of doin' things without bein' driven to it," he chuckled, as though there were some underlying humor in the observation.

"Martin would like to go," said Amelia, careful not to make her voice too eager. She set the coffee on to boil. Then she went to the door and stood for a moment looking down toward the wood road where the willows were drooping in early bud as delicate as a green rain.

It would be sweet going to church this Easter morning, she thought. It was a long time now since this had been a reverent custom with her. Amelia had been Roman Catholic before her marriage to Caleb Gare. There had been one Easter more blessed and more joyous than

all the others, when she had ridden across country to
church with Mark Jordan's father. She had been a girl
then—such a girl—not like her own daughters, but like
Lind Archer. Her heart caught her suddenly, and her
cheek warmed at the little disloyalty to her own flesh
and blood. No reason why Judith or Ellen should not
be like Lind. Was there none? A strange little jealousy
crept into her breast. Lind had undoubtedly gone to
church of an Easter Sunday, just as she had done—
perhaps even sung in a choir, just as she had done. Jude
and Ellen knew nothing of such things. Caleb did not
see fit to permit them to go to Yellow Post services,
where the lusty young swains of the entire country-
side gathered to worship in good weather. He had once
remarked pointedly to Amelia that, as she well knew,
little good could come of their mixing in with that lot,
and their salvation might easily prove their damnation.
Amelia had seen through his pretenses very clearly. And
she had come to regard with a bitter humor the sermons
he brought home each Sunday after he had been to Yellow Post, genially reading the text from the Bible and
giving a résumé of the minister's words as nearly as he
remembered them, all before dinner. She forgot the
sweetness of the willows and went back to the kitchen
stove with the faint tightening about the lips that was
all that was ever visible of Amelia's impatience with her
lot.

There was no sound in the kitchen save the crackling
of the wood in the stove and the little scraping of Caleb's
razor. In the loft above, she could hear the children

stirring, and she hoped they would not delay in coming down. When Caleb saw his collar it would be enough to set him off, without further vexation.

Lind was the first to come down. Amelia glanced at her quickly and saw how pretty she was in a blue silk gown that seemed to make her hair even more lustrous and her skin more delicate.

"Let me set the table for you, Mrs Gare," Lind offered.

"No—don't bother," said Amelia, in an abrupt tone that made Lind look at her in surprise. A slight flush came into Amelia's cheek. She could not understand herself for hating the girl at the moment. "You go out and see how nice it is," she hastened to add, "and Jude'll be down and set the table."

Wondering a little, Lind went out to the corral where a pair of yearlings came up to the wooden bar and reached out their muzzles to her for stroking.

Caleb finished shaving and pulled on his starched white shirt. Then he picked up the collar Amelia had laid out for him. He looked at it once and laid it down again, without a word. Amelia, stirring the porridge on the stove, prepared herself for his usual sneering comment. She was thankful Lind had gone out. But no remark came from Caleb. He left the collar where it was and passed softly into the other room.

Jude and Ellen and the boys came down one after the other and breakfast was on the table in a few minutes. Lind entered from the front doorway that looked out on the horse corral, and her silk gown billowed softly in the little breeze that came in behind her. She carried an armful of pussy willows that she had gathered in the ditch near the school house, and placed them in a basket beside the organ. Ellen gave them a glance and went into the kitchen abruptly.

"Cluttering up the house like that," she sniffed to Amelia, "Father will have something to say about her taking it on herself."

Amelia sighed. "Let him say it, then, Ellen," she replied. "Go and eat your breakfast. Tell the others to sit in. He'll not get to church if we don't eat right away."

On Sundays Caleb said grace. Meals on the other days were taken up with discussions of things on the farm. Lind and the others bowed their heads, but Judith sat upright and looked straight ahead of her. She forced herself to think of something else until Caleb had said "Amen." The thing that actually came into her mind was that he had not the Lord to thank for what they were about to receive, but *her*, and Martin, and Ellen, Amelia, and even Charlie, whose downcast face was hiding a grin.

"I'd like to take you with me this morning, Martin," said Caleb. "It'd do you a heap o' good, gettin' out among young people for a change. But I don't want you to be ashamed o' your own father, Martin."

Martin's long countenance lifted questioningly. He did not understand Caleb's remark, and before the Teacher he dared not ask. So he fell to eating his porridge again, slowly so that he should make no uncouth sound in Lind's presence.

Every one ate in silence. An expression of pained regret had come over Caleb's face when he spoke. Amelia knew what that meant. What he was about to say was designed to mortify her, she knew.

"No, Martin, you'll have to wait until some time when I have a clean collar to wear," he said slowly, mildly, almost humorously.

Amelia's face flamed. Her eyes darted to Lind to see if she had heard. But the Teacher went on serenely eating her breakfast.

Judith spoke up, in spite of Amelia's quick frown. "Well—I guess you'd have plenty of clean collars if you'd buy more than one a year," she snapped. "And send the stiff ones to Nykerk instead of expecting Ma to do 'em up."

"You're right, Jude. You're right," Caleb chuckled. "Guess I'm a little careless." He pushed his chair back and rose from the table. "Mind hitchin' up Lady, Charlie? You and me'll go to church anyway, collar or no collar." He turned his stooped back upon them and moved into the kitchen. Amelia followed him.

"Caleb—you're not going to church without a collar on?" she said in dismay.

He turned slowly and looked at her. "Think the Icelanders'll see what a fine wife you are, eh?" he asked softly. "Well—you go talk to Jude. See she looks to her manners. That young one is gettin' a sight too smart. Understand?" The sour grimace appeared on his face that Amelia was so used to seeing there. He ran his hand over his mustache as if to wipe the expression away. He put on his coat and went out of the house. Amelia was thankful he had not noticed the hump behind his coat collar.

She hurriedly set about clearing the table, and spoke to Judith in a low tone. "You must not cross him or be cheeky to him, Jude. You know he's getting old and can't stand it," she murmured, so that Lind should not hear.

"He's no older now than he ever was. He's always been as bad, and I'm through standin' for it," Jude replied promptly and in no low tone. "Seems to me I've just started growin' a brain enough to know how I hate him!"

"Judith!" cried Ellen, aghast. "Your own father!"

"He's not! I don't care if he is! I don't give a damn for him, and you shut up with your talk!" Jude cried, wheeling upon Ellen.

"Be quiet, Jude!" Amelia said calmly. "You're crazy to go on so! Before strangers!"

Lind had discreetly slipped out the front door.

"She's been that way ever since the Teacher came. As if nothing here is good enough for her any more," Ellen said tartly.

"That's not so! The Teacher has nothing to do with it. I've stood enough of his bullying of all of us. If he doesn't get a man here soon I'm going to leave!"

"Don't talk nonsense, Judith. You have no place to go," Amelia told her.

"Haven't I? You'll see!" She went on drying the dishes then without another word. Ellen's face was a study.

Lind crept under the fence of the sheep pasture and set out across the field. The scene was painful enough without Lind's further agonizing Amelia with her presence. Distressing conflicts of this kind had become increasingly common. She felt vaguely that her coming had incited Jude to greater rebellion. Lind wondered, as she had wondered time and again since her coming to Oeland, if there were any means in her power by which she might bring a little happiness into the lives of the Gares. And then in a moment, she was overwhelmed by her helplessness against the intangible thing that held them there, slaves to the land. It extended farther back than Caleb, this power, although it worked through him. Lind found herself longing for some one of her own world to talk with, some one to whom she might escape from the oppression of the Gares.

Judith surlily attended to the milking and helped Amelia with the separator, then took out Turk, one of the colts, and proceeded to break him into the saddle. The outraged animal threw her twice, while Martin looked on with a dry smile.

"I don't need to be thrown, Martin," Jude protested when she heard his rare laugh, "but I kind o' like it."

"Aw—yes you do," Martin grinned. "So does Turk."

"Well—you see if he does it again," she retorted, jumping into the saddle once more.

Lind, who had returned from her walk, came and sat on the ground beside Martin. He moved over for her deferentially, and blushed. It was a beautiful morning, full of sunshine, and with Caleb away the atmosphere on the farmstead was almost radiant. Although there was

not much change in their conduct, Lind felt a releasing
of reserve among the children, and delighted in being
with them. She stared at Judith on the plunging horse,
her amazement at the girl's dexterity increasing every
moment.

The animal reared and snorted, pawed the air with
his forelegs and tossed his mane like a black cloud. He
was a handsome colt, slender and glossy as black satin,
with a fine blazing eye. For a half hour Jude wrestled
with him, careening in mad circles about the corral, taking
near somersaults as the horse's forelegs straightened under him and his rear hoofs shot into the air time after time.
Her laugh rang out in peals, her eyes were full of mock-
ery. When she came close to the bar of the corral,
Lind could see that her wrists, about which the rein
was tightly wound, were bleeding.

"Don't you think she ought to stop, Martin?" Lind
asked anxiously.

"She wouldn't," said Martin shortly. "He's near
done."

When it was over, Jude unsaddled the panting, froth-
covered animal, and threw herself down beside Lind and
Martin.

"Nothing like a little exercise to make you feel good,"
she said, wiping her wrists. Her cheeks were deep red,
and little beads of moisture shone on her tilted upper
lip.

"You're marvelous, Judie," Lind said admiringly,
"but you did frighten me once or twice."

"Gee, it's a great day, Mart," Judith observed lightly,
"Couldn't you manage to sneak the spring wagon after

dinner and take us up to the Slough? I'd like to get
some crocuses. The air smells full of 'em."

"He'd say you was gaddin', like as not," Martin returned dubiously, but his eyes were unwontedly bright
as he leaned back on his elbows and looked on the distant horizon. "I might try, though."

Lind looked with mixed feelings from one to the other
of these two Gares. The height of their desire this precious April Sunday was to go gathering crocuses, and
simple as the wish was, they took it for granted that
somehow it would be denied.

"He'll be back from church about now. Sorry you
couldn't go, Mart?" Judith's eyes twinkled with mischief, and Martin in appreciation smiled his twisted
smile. Lind sat quietly watching the two while they
talked with random happiness about momentous small
things.

A half hour later the rattle of a cart sounded down
the road, and Martin rose quickly to unbar the gate.
Presently Caleb drove in with Charlie sitting very
straight and important beside him. It was the first
time in his life that Charlie had gone to church, and
the experience had left its mark on his face and bearing
much as a physical shock might have done. Martin, in
his quiet, perceiving way, looked at the boy as he got
out of the gig. Caleb went on to the house, leaving the
two boys to unharness.

"How'd ye like it?" Martin asked.

"I liked the singin' all right, but the rest—I dunno
as it was wuth goin' for," he said with a noncommittal
swagger, hands thrust in pockets. "But the singin'—

yeah, it was pretty good. Everybody sung. I sung."
He looked down sheepishly and kicked a pebble along
the ground. "You better go next time, Mart. There
was a lot o' guys there from up north way. An' some
girls. I didn't talk to 'em, though—I mean the guys.
Pa said not. Said they was Swedes and like to beat a
little fella like me up—huh!—I could o' licked any of
'em!"

Martin led the horse to the corral. He saw that Lind
and Jude had gone indoors. He was glad. Lind's presence was disturbing to him, he did not know why.
Charlie walked thoughtfully beside him.

"Say, Mart—does Pa think he's goin' to make us all
stay here after we get big?" he asked, frowning. He was
an undersized lad and looked up to his brother with some
respect because of his superior height. As Caleb had
always made a favorite of him, and was amused by his
heedlessness, he had nothing but contempt for his sisters
who had been trained never to disobey their father or
to speak impudently to him.

"Well, I'm big, Charlie, ain't I? I guess like as not
we'll all stay," Martin replied soberly. So now Charlie
was beginning to wonder, too, he thought.

Charlie was silent as they went to the house. He was
only fifteen, it was true. But to-day he had heard sing-
ing, and had found he liked to sing, with a lot of young
folks like himself or a little older. There was one boy
there he would have liked to talk to. The boy had a red
tie, and put collection in the plate from his own pocket.

Before dinner on Sunday it was the custom for the
family to assemble in the sitting room and hear Caleb

recite the sermon that had been delivered at Yellow
Post church. Although for reasons of his own he did
not think it well to permit the family to go to the service, he felt that it was unbefitting a Christian to keep
them from the grace of God's word.

"Will you join us in hearing the sermon, Miss Archer?"
Caleb asked the Teacher when Amelia was drawing the
chairs into a semicircle in the middle of the room. His
manner was his best, suave, gentle and benevolent. He
had taken the Bible down from its place on the shelf
above the organ, and held it a little distance away from
him as he had seen the new preacher do, as if not to
desecrate the book by contact with his sinfully mortal
person.

Lind could not well refuse. She sat down with the
others, and Ellen at the organ played *Lead, Kindly Light*.
Then Caleb held up a hand and intoned the Lord's
prayer. His voice was miraculously soft. Suddenly
Lind found herself wanting to cry out against the farce,
and confront Caleb with the monstrousness of his act.
But she sat silent.

Caleb opened the Bible and read:

*"Again, I considered all travail, and every right work,
that for this a man is envied of his neighbor. This is
also vanity and vexation of spirit.*

*"The fool foldeth his hands together, and eateth his
own flesh.*

*"Better is an handful in quietness, than both the hands
full with travail and vexation of spirit.*

"Then I returned, and I saw vanity under the sun."

Caleb paused, cleared his throat, and looked significantly at each member of the family, dwelling last upon Lind. The Teacher stirred with discomfort under the steely condemnation in the old man's eyes. His voice went on, rising to a grand sonorousness:

"There is one alone, and there is not a second; yea, he has neither child nor brother: yet is there no end of all his labor; neither is his eye satisfied with riches; neither saith he, For whom do I labor, and bereave my soul of good? This is vanity, yea, it is a sore travail.

"Two are better than one; because they have a good reward for their labor.

"For if they fall, the one will lift his fellow: but woe to him that is alone when he falleth; for he hath not another to help him up.

"Again, if two lie together, then they have heat: but how can one be warm alone?

"And if one prevail against him, two shall withstand him; and a threefold cord is not quickly broken."

Caleb sternly closed the book. "So endeth the lesson," he said huskily.

The children, waiting for the end of the ordeal, had only half heard the words. But Amelia, naturally pious, had drunk them in. One phrase stuck in her mind. "The fool foldeth his hands together, and eateth his own flesh." That was what he was doing. That was what she was helping him do. Eating his own flesh, here on the land. But for her there was no alternative, no choice save which of her flesh she should eat. O God, it was

unendurable!   Caleb was going on—and on—the sermon
—the new preacher's sermon . . .

"So must we, who dwell in this lonely land and strive
to live Christian lives on the acres the Lord hath given
us, cling together for warmth and for good reward for our
labor.   'Better is an handful with quietness, than both
the hands full with travail and vexation of spirit.'
Better live here like we are, poor but content, than to seek
the world and all its vices for enlargement of our worldly
wealth.   That, Jude, is for you to think of, careful, and
for you, Ellen and Martin, and like as not, for you,
Charlie.   'For if they fall, the one will lift up his fellow:
but *woe*'—hear me—'*woe* to him that is alone when he
falleth.'   Do they understand the lesson, Amelia?"

Amelia murmured, "Yes, I think they all understand
it."   She could have shouted aloud, beaten his face for
his hypocrisy.   She could have risen and belabored him
with all her strength for his bland misappropriation of a
noble passage from the book that had given her many an
hour's comfort.   But she did nothing but sit and listen
attentively until he had, in a hushed voice, given the
last blessing.

"This was not strictly an Easter Sunday sermon, you
understand.   But Reverend Blossom thought it more like
for us to have a sermon that would fit in with the season,
so he said.   What do you think, Amelia?"

"I think it was a well chosen sermon," said Amelia
quietly.

Then they all rose and sat down at the table, while Mrs
Gare brought the food from the kitchen, and Judith,
yawning with boredom, helped her.

3

On the following Friday, Gertrude Bjarnasson, who
had been friendly toward Ellen the time or two that she
had talked with her at Yellow Post, invited Ellen and the
Teacher for a visit, sending the message to them through
the younger children who went to school. Ellen made
so bold as to ask Caleb for permission to accompany
Lind to the great stone house of the Icelanders on the
lake.

Caleb regarded her with pained surprise.

"Do you want them to show you their fine house, and
their fishing nets, and their boats, and their windmill,
when your own father is too poor to have such things?
You know how much better they think they are than us,"
he said gently, wagging his head, "but if you *must*
go . . ."

Ellen sighed. She had never been at the great stone
house. She would never, perhaps, be permitted to go.
But it was of no use to protest—Amelia would be seen
weeping a short time afterward if she did. There was
nothing to do but bear with things. And wonder if Malcolm would ever be coming back again. He had said—
ah, yes, he had said that he would, in the spring.

It was just a year since Malcolm had left to work in the
lumber mills to the south. And before that there had
been only a week or two of incomprehensible, guilty rap-
ture. Malcolm had kissed Ellen but once when they were
alone in the barn after milking. An unromantic place it
was save for the witching flood of light from a full moon.
It had been a moment of unforgettable bliss. Had Mal-

colm been less diffident that evening, had he seized the opportunity and taken her away before she had time to re-
flect, everything would have been different. But Ellen,
sustained by her habitual loyalty to Caleb and by the fact
that Malcolm had Indian blood in his veins, regained over-
night her unbendable control, and Malcolm, wounded
and perplexed, went away soon afterward. It was only
the pain in her eyes that prompted him to tell her that he
would be coming back again. And here it was spring—
after the long winter. . . .

So, without Ellen, Lind went home that Friday evening with the children of the Bjarnassons, the great clan
who lived to the westward.

The air was soft and vibrant with the whir of migra-
tory wild fowl. Rain pools filled the ditches along the
road, and lay like stained glass in the low sun; the overhanging willows were in full leaf now, the sedges vividly
green and as yet unbowed by a single wind. Such a new,
ecstatic world of growth! Behind the Bjarnasson children in the cart, Lind held out her hands as if to gather
in the beauty of it from the wide air.

In the great stone house on the lake, dwelt four gener-
ations of Bjarnassons. Old Erik, who was among the
first of the Icelanders to settle at Oeland, had seen his
land pass in turn from his son to his son's son. Erik was
well into his eighties now, a time for dreaming much, and
fishing a little when the sun was warm on the white rocks
in the cove. Young Erik, his grandson, had married long
since and now sent his children to Oeland School. It was
young Erik's father, Mathias, who had built the stone
house.

Mathias was a massive man, sixty now, but eternal in endurance, eternal in warmth and hospitality of nature. The house he had built with his own hands was like him, was a square stone image of him. He had excavated the earth and built its rugged, lasting foundation; had hauled stones in slow wagon-loads, and with the care and fineness of a woman patterning lace, had fitted them together in the mortar and had built four broad walls to the blue.

In all that region, there was not another house like it.

Like a welcome, its western windows were aflame with light from a red sun, when Andres and Helga drove up the road with the Teacher. Below the house lay the lake, wrought through and through with silver and rose.

Helga escorted Lind into the house.

The immaculate kitchen had a warm, good smell, like cinnamon. The floor was white as bread. On it were round, braided rag mats of bright, clear colors.

Helga's mother had never been in Iceland, but her English was so little used that it halted here and there. Such was the isolation of the place.

"You will like coffee, now, maybe," she said to Lind, half shyly. "Bring the teacher a chair, Helga."

She hurried about, a round little figure of a woman with a round, unchanging face. From an immense wooden cupboard with red glass doors she brought out cups and saucers, and certain thin wafers rolled up tightly in sugar. And while Lind ate and drank, she sat with her hands clasped in her lap, saying never a word.

From an inner room, Lind heard a steady, muffled sound, between a hum and a purr.

"It is grandmother, spinning," said Mrs Bjarnasson. "She is blind, but she spins. She spins all of our wool."

"She speaks no English, of course," said Lind.

She spoke none. But when Lind went in and shook hands with her, the ancient lady raised her face to hers as if she were looking at her with recognition. She was so stooped that as she sat at the spinning wheel, her head was almost level with the distaff.

She murmured something in Icelandic.

"She means that you are good to look on," said Mrs Bjarnasson the younger. "She always says she can see people's faces when they speak the first time to her. She will tell your fortune if you ask her."

Lind was eager to hear the old lady, who drew aside from her spinning and took both of the Teacher's hands in her own withered ones. She held them and turned her knotted, brown face, that had something of the sheen of a cocoon, upward to the light, her eyes sealed.

She spoke rapidly, in a queer, lilting voice. The younger Mrs Bjarnasson interpreted as she went along.

"She says you will have a lover very soon," Lind was told. "There is a shadow over him. You will never know the secret of him. But you will be happy. That is all—that is enough, she has told you."

Lind laughed, but a ripple crossed her heart.

"Does she always tell the truth?" the Teacher asked.

"Wait and see," said Mrs Bjarnasson, nodding her head.

Superstition here lay along life in a broad vein.

The men came in to supper from work in the fields and along the shore: young Erik's brothers, Peter and Valdemar, and his cousin, Johan; Mathias, laughing mightily at some joke he had turned on one of them.

They spoke in the Icelandic, simple and rough, not thinking to change in deference to the Teacher. They spoke no ill: why should they affect a strange tongue to prove it? Each greeted Lind with an awkward politeness. The women of the family they each kissed in turn. It was the custom.

There were other women in the family as well: Gertrude and Althea, sisters of young Erik, and Althea, his maiden aunt. The women were in constant attendance upon Lind, to see that she was at ease. While supper was being prepared the elder Althea, who was somewhat intellectual, brought her a book of Icelandic sagas translated into English, and placed a stool under her feet to insure her comfort: then she moved as quietly away as a wraith.

The supper was a vast affair of fish that had been brought from the "great" river, dried meats, potatoes, and many kinds of crisp sugared cakes, and many cups of coffee. The men ate heartily of the fish, greatly of the potatoes. To Lind it was a revelation.

A wind rose suddenly before the meal was over, and in a surprisingly short time the lake was breaking in a long shudder against the rocky shore. Quiet descended upon the family group, as though from some unseen force outside.

"Baldur will not rest to-night," the elder Althea murmured in the language. Her eyes were bright and strangely young, although she was fifty and had never married.

"Baldur was a fool to defy the lake that night. He will be a long time on the bottom," grunted the younger Erik. But he started as a door slammed shut in the upper part of the house.

"Tell the Teacher," Gertrude said. She was round-eyed and pretty. She had stared uninterruptedly at Lind throughout the meal. Now there was a detached look in her face.

"The Teacher has heard, like as not," began young Erik, in the uneven vowel tones of the Icelander. "The Gares know, I think."

"No," said Lind. "I have not heard anything."

"The lake has two of our family. One, my brother, Gisli, one my sister Althea's promised husband. They were friends, and they quarreled. They carried their quarrel into the lake in two boats. It was a storm— the lake took them. We have not yet found any of them—not a small sign. Until so, we do not let others fish in the lake. Caleb Gare, he says, yes, he shall fish. We say no. We are a family, Mees Archer—a great family. We shall not let others in to fish where our dead is buried." Young Erik ended sternly.

The wind and water screamed against the shore. Lind trembled, and thrilled.

"No, they will not rest until we find them," said the elder Althea. Her niece and namesake sat still with her eyes downcast.

There followed tales of supernatural events, of visions and omens, and of disaster that befell the unheeding. The great, grizzled Mathias told solemnly of the ancient pride of the Bjarnassons in Iceland, and of the dire fate

of one who was disloyal to that pride, to that great bond.
Told of how the curse of the ancients fell upon him,
and of how his days were a torment and his nights a
madness, so that even death could not bring forgetfulness.
There was a weird poetry in Mathias' telling, a great
rhythm of melancholy romance. He had lived much in
communion with solitude, and had come to know that
there is an unmeasurable Alone surrounding each soul,
and that nameless and undreamed are the forms that drift
within that region. So that it was well for the members
of a great family to cleave together and so ward off the
menaces and the dreads of the great Alone.

When the Teacher went to bed finally, the storm had
abated. High above the soughing of the wind under
the great eaves of the stone house, Lind heard the trail-
ing clangor of the wild geese. Their cry smote upon the
heart like the loneliness of the universe . . . a magnificent seeking through solitude—an endless quest.

4

The farm of Thorvald Thorvaldson lay half-way between the Gares' and the Bjarnassons'.

Thorvald had nine girls, and no boys. Consequently
his farm was a fragment of neglect, a ragged piece of
land of no value save as a hindrance to Caleb Gare's
ambition to extend his pastures farther westward.
Which hindrance, Thorvald maintained, was gratifying in
itself.

Lind stopped there on her way home from the Bjarnassons' to speak to Mrs Thorvaldson about the condition

of the scalps of her younger daughters.   She would bring the matter up delicately.

From the seat of the Bjarnasson children's cart, Lind saw Mrs Thorvaldson struggling with the cattle in the milk yard—saw her pushed and jostled about by the unmanageable animals, which she was trying to separate. Lind saw also that she was heavy with child.

Somehow, Lind could not bring herself to mention the heads.   She waved good morning to the woman and then told Andres to drive back to the road.   She herself would use kerosene on the young ones.

From the top of the sharp ridge that looked down upon the forks where three roads met, from the north, the east and the west, Lind saw a man on horseback. His head was bare, his hat slung across the pommel of his saddle.   His clothes, the contour of his well-groomed head, even the way he sat astride his horse signified to Lind that he was from the world beyond Nykerk Siding, from the direction of which he had come.   For some reason she felt shy about encountering him, and asked Andres to rein in and let the stranger pass ahead of them on the forks.   Andres stopped the horse, and Lind was confident that the man on horseback rode on without having seen them.

5

Mark Jordan smiled to himself as he jogged along the road on the Indian pony he had hired at the Siding to take him to the farm of the Hungarian, Anton Klovacz. His greenish, ironical eyes, that could in an instant take on the shadow of a dream, searched the dust in the road ahead of him, and saw never the track or trace of human passage. For a day, then, fully, the road had been empty save, perhaps, for the foraging sparrows. What an ideal place to come to, away from Arbuthnot and his wife and their eternal friends, who would leave their tracks on pavement, if self-importance counted for anything. But then—perhaps he was unfair. Arbuthnot wasn't such a rotter in some ways. But he did get on the nerves of a man whose nerves were raw to begin with—with his ever-lasting talk on art and the City Beautiful of To-morrow. A good architect, in his way, but an unbearable ass. No better as an architect than Mark himself, if it came to that, for all his name and fame. Well, he was free of it all for a half year, thanks to good old Doc Brisbane! There was a medico with perception! One who could tell what the soul of a man wanted long before the body tumbled to it, fret about as it might in the quest.

God, how good this air was! It smelt like the young lilac leaves you used to suck against your lips and break with a snap when you were a kid, or like the slippery elm bark you used to chew and make a viscous cud of!

Dwelling on his childhood, Mark thought of the kindly old priests in the mission who had given him everything in the way of training and education in the hope that his mind would develop along religious lines. If they had harbored any resentment, they had concealed it well, and had encouraged him when he took early to archi-tecture. He would have to go back and visit them when this "jump cure" as old Brisbane called it, was effected.

Mark paused in the road and looked out over the prairie, flat and new looking, as though hills had not yet been dreamt of by its Creator. On the north side of the road there was stiff timber, scantily green as yet, springing up from ground that was black and scarred from an old fire. Mark dismounted and stepped in among the charred stumps of the old trees. At the base of one, leaning against it as if for shelter, grew a tiny wood violet, almost colorless. He looked at it but did not pluck it as he was first tempted to do. He laughed at himself for his compassion and walked back to his horse.

"We all do that—lean up against burnt stumps—somehow or other," he mused. And then he wondered, rather relevantly, he thought, "What would have happened to me if mother and father had lived?"

As he rode along, a mood of loneliness overtook him— the same cold feeling of belonging nowhere that he had had at night when he was a little boy, after the priest had put the light out and he lay listening to the rain on the glass of the window. He shook himself impatiently. Time he was getting over that morose habit now, nearing thirty. He looked over his shoulder and saw that the sun made only a fillip of gold on the rim of the horizon. A steady blue was creeping over the prairie in place of the magnificent light that had been there the moment before. The churr of the frogs had begun in the ditches along the road, and the small leaves on the willows hung with a faint indolence. Suddenly Mark stopped his horse to listen. He lifted his face up to catch the strange sound that was passing over him, a great summoning trumpet-call, that seemed to hollow out the heavens.

"Wild geese," he said aloud. "They sound as if they know something about it—something about being alone."

CHAPTER III

1

On a morning ringing with bird-song, Ellen and Martin took the wagon into the "bush" for wood. It was before school time, an hour after sunrise, and the Teacher, who always breakfasted, of course, with the family, rode with them.

When the horse came to a stand, Lind asked Ellen and Martin to listen. In the stillness among the dogwood trees the first sunlight lay like a faint yellow dust. Suddenly a cat-bird called. Lind trilled, whistled. The cat-bird returned the salute on the identical note. Lind laughed. There was a birdish laugh from the trees.

"We used to do that when we were kids," said Ellen. "A long time ago——"

"Remember that blue-jay we saw, Ellen? That one that was mad at the cat-birds," Martin put in. There was something almost eager in his voice.

Ellen laughed her half-startled laugh. She did everything suddenly, nervously, after a period of slow considering.

Lind followed them into the timber, where Martin fell to with the ax, cleaving with sloping blows into the bole of a dry birch. The swing and shock of the ax broke into the cool morning and woke a chorus of echoes. While Martin chopped, Lind helped Ellen drag the trees, which were small, into a clearing. Then Ellen, with a hatchet, trimmed them down to the trunk. Afterward they piled them into the wagon, and saw that the sun was now free of the bush and that it must be well on toward nine o'clock. Before Ellen returned to the wagon the last time she ran a thorn through her shoe and into her foot. But she said nothing about it. Ellen had come to pride herself on her stoic endurance of physical pain, and no matter how small or great it was, pain was no longer distinguished for her by its degree.

Martin was happy this morning. Lind saw that he was, and would have liked to engage him in conversation about himself, but knew his shyness.

It always made him happy to feel his strength where results were immediate. He did not know, however, that this was the cause of his mood. He would have whistled, or even stamped with both feet on the floor of the wagon had the Teacher not been there.

Caleb Gare was inspecting a number of cattle in the barn-yard when Martin and Ellen returned. They had left the Teacher at the school.

Caleb called to Martin.

"These steers go in to the Siding to-morrow. Take Ellen with you."

Martin wondered to himself what object there was in selling steers just now, but he said nothing. Then he noticed that one of the animals was a favorite of Judith's, which she had raised and planned to sell in the fall in order to purchase a winter coat. Still he made no comment. It was Judith's steer. . . .

That day Ellen applied poultices of hot soaked bread to her foot. Amelia was concerned about it, but, as was her way, made no mention of it to Caleb when he came in for the noon meal.

Charlie had given Amelia further cause for distress that morning. He had ridden the mare so hard that she had come home in a white froth: and Charlie knew it was forbidden to spend the animal in such a way. The mare was still quivering in the stable when Caleb examined her. It happened that Judith had just returned from the muskeg where, mounted on Prince, she had roped out a calf that had broken from the pasture with a number of cows.

Caleb entered the house. Amelia, busily taking biscuits from the oven for dinner, saw his face and knew that something had happened. Ellen's foot and now trouble over the mare. Amelia pushed her hair back from her hot forehead.

"Where is Judith?" Caleb demanded, the points of his eyes fixed.

Ellen, who was setting the table, straightened her narrow back and listened. So Judith, thoughtless of Amelia, had done something again.

"She's putting ointment on her hands," Amelia said.

"And well she might! Ointment! T—t—ch! Bring her here!"

"What is it, Caleb? What has she done?"

"Done! Bring her here, I say!" The veins in his neck swelled to livid welts. Amelia hurried past him to call Jude from the loft, but the girl had heard the conversation where she stood upstairs.

She came into the kitchen, her hands hanging before her and covered with yellow salve where the rope with which she had rescued the calf had burned into the flesh. She regarded Caleb coldly.

"Well?" she asked.

Caleb approached her, his head jutting forward from his shoulders.

"Don't you 'well' me! What have you done with the mare? What have you done with her, I say?" His voice rose from a sort of husky whisper to a thin peal.

"I wasn't riding the mare!"

"Then who had her? Who had her but you—tell me that."

"Charlie rode the mare, Caleb! I told him before he took her out to be easy with her," Amelia put in hurriedly.

Caleb threw back his head with a jerk. He laughed. *"You* did! Well, well!"

Laughing softly, he shuffled into the other room and sat down to the table. Presently the others came in and quietly took their places. When Lind entered and threw her wide lacy hat upon the hair sofa, Amelia winced at the incongruity of her presence in the room. The Teacher smiled at them all and sat down in her chair.

"It's the most beautiful day we have had yet this spring," she remarked. "I have never seen the sky so blue or the trees so green. The rain last night seems to have cleared the whole world. It must have been fine for the crops, Mr Gare?"

"Hm—yes, yes indeed. So she threw you, eh, Charlie?" Caleb asked the boy, scarcely glancing at Lind in reply to her question. He winked at Charlie and Charlie grinned broadly. The youngest of the Gares had an habitual snuffle which Amelia had tried in vain to correct. He was an anæmic looking boy, and cared little for anything except that which was forbidden. This trait appealed to Caleb, and he chose to humor it, to the annoyance and indignation of the others, especially Judith. Charlie had always taken advantage of his father's leniency.

"Nix," said Charlie. "She smelt a bear. The Klovaczs shot at two last night—one got away with a pig."

"Bears, eh? That means trouble," Caleb observed, to switch the subject. "Have to look out on the way to Nykerk to-morrow, Martin. Keep Ellen under cover. She's nice and plump. Eh, Ellen?" He leaned over and playfully tweaked Ellen's arm. She smiled, dutifully. Judith made a grimace which she did not try to hide.

To the end of the meal Caleb was genial, jovial, in fact. No further mention was made of the mare. Judith had not ridden her, after all.

2

For the rest of that day, Judith's hands were of no use to her, so she slipped away with her dog, Pete, through the bush to a little ravine where a pool had gathered below the thread of a spring. Pete caught a scent and was off, and Judith was left alone.

It was clingingly warm, as before rain. Not knowing fully what she was doing, Judith took off all her clothing and lay flat on the damp ground with the waxy feeling of new, sunless vegetation under her. She needed to escape, to fly from something—she knew not what. Caleb . . . Ellen . . . the farm, the hot reek of manure in the stable when it was close as to-day. Life was smothering, overwhelming her, like a pillow pressed against her face, like a feather tick pinning down her body.

She would have struck Caleb to-day had it not been for Amelia. Always pity stood in the way of the tide of violence she felt could break from her. Pity for Amelia, who would get what Caleb did not dare mete out to her, Judith.

Oh, how knowing the bare earth was, as if it might have a heart and a mind hidden here in the woods. The fields that Caleb had tilled had no tenderness, she knew. But here was something forbiddenly beautiful, secret as one's own body. And there was something beyond this. She could feel it in the freeness of the air, in the depth of the earth. Under her body there were, she had been taught, eight thousand miles of earth. On the other side, what? Above her body there were leagues and leagues of air, leading like wings—to what? The marvelous confusion and complexity of all the world had singled her out from the rest of the Gares. She was no longer one of them. Lind Archer had come and her delicate fingers had sprung a secret lock in Jude's being. She had opened like a tight bud. There was no going back now into the darkness.

Sven Sandbo, he would be home in May, so they said. Was it Sven she wanted, now that she was so strangely free? Judith looked straight above her through the network of white birch and saw the bulbous white country

that a cloud made against the blue. Something beyond
Sven, perhaps . . . Freedom, freedom. She dipped her
blistered hands down into the clear topaz of the pool,
lifted them and dipped them and lifted them, letting
the drops slip off the tips of her fingers each time like
tiny cups of light. She thought of the Teacher, of her
dainty hands and her soft, laughing eyes . . . she came
from another life, another world. She would go back
there again. Her hands would never be maps of blisters
as Jude's were now, from tugging a calf out of a mud-
hole. Jude hid her hands behind her and pressed her
breast against the cold ground. Hard, senseless sobs
rose in her throat, and her eyes smarted with tears. She
was ugly beyond all bearing, and all her life was ugly.
Suddenly she was bursting with hatred of Caleb. Her
large, strong body lay rigid on the ground, and was
suddenly unnatural in that earthy place. Then she relaxed and wept like a woman. . . .

3

Judith dressed, whistled to Pete, and when he came
bounding joyously toward her, walked slowly back home.
On the way she passed the north cow-pasture where Caleb
kept a few bull-calves among the milch cows. She
leaned against the fence and looked in at two of the
plump young bulls who were dancing about and playfully
skulling each other, having apparently just discovered
their sprouting horns. She saw how they had developed
since she had last observed them. Their grizzled, stupid
faces had become more surly, their flanks heavier, their

dewlaps smoother and whiter and thicker. Caleb would soon be ringing their noses, and they would become spiritlessly ugly, with all this madcap frenzy suppressed. They were beautiful bulls, and would bring a nice sum from one of the Icelanders, perhaps. Judith felt an inner excitement in watching them. She turned to go, feeling dismayed that she should be so attracted by the young beasts. But a curiosity over which she had no control held her there for many minutes. Ah, how violent they were becoming in their play. . . .

Judith heard Charlie crashing through the timber on his horse, calling the cattle. With the dog at her heels she fled home.

Ellen was examining her foot when Jude came into the house.

"I can take the cattle with Martin to-morrow, Ellen," Jude said sympathetically. "Your foot looks like it's spavined."

"It'll be all right in the morning, I hope," Ellen replied. "Father wants me to go."

"Huh!" Judith retorted. "And you'd go, too,—on crutches!"

"Hush, girls!" Amelia pleaded. "Let's not have any more trouble to-night. The mare's enough for one day."

However, when Caleb came in from the stable, Judith took pains to mention to Ellen again her willingness to go in her place. The Teacher, working at her desk at the other end of the room, watched Caleb out of the corner of her eye. She made a little wager with herself that he would appear not to have heard Judith. She won the wager.

After a moment, Caleb, looking up from his agriculture journal, called loudly to Amelia who was in the kitchen.

"Heard to-day that Sven Sandbo's comin' up from the Siding to-morrow," he said.

Jude's color rose at once. Ellen glanced at her. Both knew, as did the Teacher, that he had not been off the farm all day and could not possibly have heard such a thing, no one having stopped in.

A little later, after he had talked casually on other things, he turned to Judith and said, "You can use the new harrow on the east garden to-morrow, Jude."

"Ellen can't go with Martin the way her foot is," Judith observed.

"You mean, Jude, not if Sven Sandbo is coming up from Nykerk. Hah! Hah! Caught you that time!" He laughed heartily, passing his hand across his mustache. His eyes gleamed with open-hearted mischief. How he loved to have sport with the girls on the subject of beaux! "You're too young to be moonin', Jude. I notice it in you lately. Haven't you, Miss Archer?"

Lind smiled at Judith, who sprang up, furious. Caleb regarded her with amusement.

"Mother, I'm afraid Jude is forgetting herself." He turned and chuckling almost inaudibly went out once more on one of his mysterious inspections about the place.

"Oh, Jude, you know what that always means!" Ellen whispered so Lind should not hear. "Why on earth can't you control yourself?"

But Judith was sitting dumb and somber at the window, looking out into the twilight. In a few minutes she got up and began to help Amelia with the supper.

"I wish we could stop eating once in a while," Amelia sighed. "It gets tiresome."

Caleb did not come in at all for supper. Everyone, even Lind, knew the significance of that. After the children had gone to bed he would be heard talking in a low tone to Amelia, and in the morning her eyes would be ringed with shadows. During the meal, Ellen looked across the table at Judith with the rebuke that the younger girl had come to hate. Judith bolted her food and went upstairs.

When Caleb returned indoors it was to announce bed time. He did so pleasantly, but Amelia saw below his pleasantness. The children and Lind went to the loft. Caleb was the clock by which the family slept, woke, ate and moved.

"Five in the morning, everybody. Ellen and Martin are going to take the steers in to Nykerk, remember," he called after them.

4

Everyone, including Lind, to whom the tyranny was rather novel, was at breakfast at half past five.

There was this to be said about the enforced early rising: you saw the unbelievable dawn whether you wished to or not. It unfolded like a vast flower over the edge of the horizon. The earth was clear and dark under it, as if seen through blue glass. One was aware for the first time of standing on a sphere that moved rhythmically through space. It was an hour of crystal-clear perceptions.

But breakfast was a bleak affair. Ellen was pale from the pain in her foot, and Amelia torn between mother solicitude and the submission she had learned through her trying wifehood. Caleb and Martin talked about the sale of the cattle; no mention was made of Judith's steer, although Martin resolved to see that she was given one in its place.

Judith sullenly hurried out after she had had a cup of coffee, and began to pitch manure into the cart. Her hands were still swollen and sore, but pride kept her from complaining. If Ellen could stand it for Amelia's sake, she could.

Ellen and Martin drove away with the steers before the Teacher could say good-by to them.

She ran out and watched them disappear down the road, Martin stooped over on the wagon seat like an old, tired man, Ellen sitting rather too stiff to be natural.

And Caleb Gare left to attend a business meeting of the church at Yellow Post. Although it took time from his own affairs, it pleased him to be one of the trustees of the church, as he was of the school. The pleasure came mainly from seeing that none of the other guardians of the church funds abused the trust placed in them.

It was because he had a little suspicion concerning Bjorn Aronson, who was treasurer of the church funds, that he went to the meeting that particular day.

He watched the younger brother of Fusi Aronson narrowly throughout the meeting, in which it was taken for granted that the money Bjorn was entrusted with lay safely in the strong box at the Aronson farm. Caleb saw no reason why Bjorn, at this time of the year, should have been able to buy three head of pure bred Jersey cattle from that infidel, Klovacz, who did not even belong to the church. Caleb had singled out the new cattle in the herd, and had recognized them at once.

After the meeting he stepped up behind Bjorn, who was untying his horses from the hitching post.

"See you have some Jerseys," he said, tapping the young man on the shoulder. Bjorn started. Caleb smiled.

"Ya–a, sure," said Bjorn.

"Get 'em at the Siding?"

"Naa–ow. Bought from Klovacz. He needed the money, before he goes avay," Bjorn said. His eyes traveled down the road. Caleb smiled again, balancing back on his heels thoughtfully. Bjorn got into his wagon and drove down toward Yellow Post proper, giving his horses the whip.

Bjorn was not the man his brother was, but because Fusi was honest Oeland took it that good blood ran all the way through the family. There they made their little mistake, Caleb thought, congratulating himself upon having discovered a stain upon the Aronson escutcheon which he might with ease lay his finger on. No, he had long known that Bjorn was not the boy his brother was. Bjorn had not even troubled to learn English with the pains that Fusi had given to it. Caleb would pay a little visit to Fusi on the way home, he decided.

There was another little matter that Caleb thought it would be advantageous to attend to. He got into his cart, clucked to the horse and headed him in the direction of the Klovacz homestead. The day was pleasant and Caleb was in an exceedingly good humor. By turning his head westward he could look upon his own fields, already green and promising. On the east lay the straggling, stony land of Anton Klovacz, with his few acres of miserable timothy. He laughed at the irony that lay in Mark Jordan's coming to this morose patch of land, all that Anton Klovacz, with rarest good luck pending upon the granting of the government title, would leave in his will a few short months hence!

Caleb turned into the narrow, infrequently-used wood road that led past Anton Klovacz's outbuildings. He drove slowly, and let the wheels run on the grass alongside, so that there should be as little sound as possible from them. He craned his neck to see all that he could of the Klovacz place.

It was months since he had talked with Anton, but he had heard at Yellow Post that the man was failing fast and was leaving very soon for the city where a great specialist was to examine him. But that news only corroborated the statement of Bart Nugent, who in his last letter had told Caleb that Mark Jordan was leaving at once to tend to Klovacz's homestead during his absence. Bart was a clever man, and he had done Caleb a life-long service, never suspecting to what purpose. Bart had fondly thought that Caleb had Mark's interest at heart because of Amelia. A veterinary surgeon and a keeper of stables, Bart had managed to continue his acquaintance with Mark Jordan in a friendly fashion even after the war, and had faithfully reported every move that the young man made. Caleb chuckled to himself when he reviewed the situation. Bart had been a good sort. But now——

Caleb removed his last letter from his vest pocket, together with the one from the hospital which had forwarded it to him. He shook his head, and a look came into his eyes that was seldom seen there. It was the look of the old when they hear of the passing of the old. Amelia must never learn that Bart Nugent was gone. For it was Bart and his assiduous reporting on Mark that she feared. Bart was Caleb's only connection with the outer world. Even if Amelia did learn of Mark's presence on the Klovacz farm, she must never know that Bart Nugent was dead. Mark Jordan would return to the city, and Caleb would lose all trace of him, but that Amelia must never know. For that would mean an end to Amelia's fear.

Caleb skulked along in the cart, close to the alder bushes that were flowering like creamy curds between the road and the Klovacz farm. He heard the voices of two men who were approaching on the opposite side of the fence. One voice was reedy and high as a child's, almost with the thin wail of wind in a chimney; the other was rich and controlled, full of another kind of youth. Caleb at once hated the deep assurance in the second voice. He knew by instinct that it was Mark Jordan's. The other was that of Anton Klovacz, dying of consumption with his feet on government soil.

Through the thick weave of the bushes, Caleb caught a glimpse of the two men. Jordan was tall and broad, Anton Klovacz still taller and as narrow as a pine board. His shoulders were scoop-shaped, his face all gone to cheek bones and hollows. "God, how he looks!" said

Caleb to himself. Disease—destruction—things that he feared—things out of man's control.

As the men passed, Caleb turned his head and followed the form of Mark Jordan until his eyes ached from the strain. Pah, how like his father he was—walking like he was God Almighty! The furious jealousy of Caleb's earlier years came into his heart again like a ravaging disease long checked and now broken out more violently than ever. Bareheaded, he sat in the cart with his long arms stretched rigid down between his knees, his hands clasped together. The reins hung loose, the horse pawed impatiently at the ground. A cat-bird in the nearest alder-bush made a querying little sound. But Caleb sat on, oblivious to all about him. Not his son, not his son, that handsome lad! The son of Amelia and big Del Jordan, who was gored by a bull. Caleb's sons —Caleb's children, what were they? Well born, it was true, and not out of wedlock. But twisted and gnarled and stunted as the growth on the bush land he owned, and barren as had been his acres before he had put his own life's blood into them for a meager yield. Caleb's head slipped down until his chin touched his chest. The soft wind moved in his scrag of hair, and in the invisible touch was a gesture of infinite pity.

5

Caleb turned into the farmyard of Fusi Aronson. His face was lined with hard mirth. He had come upon a choice errand. The great Icelander strode down to meet him, and bade him a stiff good day.

"I hear Bjorn has bought some cattle from Klovacz," Caleb began smoothly, dismounting from the cart. "He must be well off this spring."

"It was in settlement of a debt Klovacz owed him," Fusi replied shortly.

Caleb laughed. "Oh, no, it wasn't, Fusi. Klovacz got good money in return for those same Jerseys."

Fusi started. "What do you mean, Mr Gare?"

Caleb stepped closer to the Icelander and lifted his eyebrows meaningly.

"Of course he'll put the money back in the strong box, Fusi. The church needs it, you know," he said gently, laying his finger on the bib of the big man's overalls. He turned to go.

"Of course," he added, "you needn't fear that *I'm* goin' to squeal."

Fusi, in his heavy way, was looking at him uncertainly, not quite grasping the thing. Then the slow red surged up into his face. He knotted his huge fists and plunged toward Caleb.

"Take your time, Fusi, take your time," Caleb mocked. "Look in the strong box first. And by the way, when you are ready to deal with me about that timber down there between my hayfields, let me know. The sooner the better for me."

He mounted the cart and drove away.

CHAPTER IV

1

THE three black-eyed Klovacz children no longer brought crocuses and violets to Lind on the May mornings. Their father, Anton Klovacz, was seriously ill, Lind was told. And because there was no mother in the family, all the children left with him in the covered wagon for the city in the south, where a great physician would be called into attendance. Anton's savings would go, of course.

He had hired a man to look after his live-stock during his absence, the children informed Lind on their last day at school. He was a very nice, strong man, they said, who had brought them candy from the city and had let them search his pockets and keep all the silver they found there. On the very first day they had got so well acquainted with him that the younger of them had scrambled all over him in a free-for-all tumble, until they finally got him on his back on the ground, where he lay laughing heartily.

A few days later he had gone to Yellow Post and had brought back a box that sang and made music. It had been sent to him from the city from which he had come. A number of books with shiny leather covers had come, too, but the children couldn't make out a word of them, or at least not a whole line anywhere. Whoever the man was, it was plain that the children had been won over by him completely.

The evenings were now so marvelously tender that Lind could not tolerate the imprisoned feeling on the Gare farm. She made a habit of going on long cross-country tramps alone, after school, returning barely in time for supper. She rarely met anyone, either driving or on foot, to detract from the lonely charm of her jaunts. Wondering a little about the man from the city who had come to the Klovacz place, she had several times been tempted to walk over that way. Of course he would be only a laborer, and would doubtless not be bothered with talking to her, but merely a glimpse of him would restore her confidence that the world she had come from was still in existence.

One day the Sandbo children left their pony for her to ride. The evening set in with a fine gray web of rain, and Lind dressed in rough clothes, mounted the pony and rode southeast, toward the Klovacz homestead. She took the narrow, winding trail that Caleb had driven on not long before. She passed the alder bushes and came to a stretch where the chokecherry trees on either side bowed toward each other and almost shut out the sky.

On the road Lind met a man, walking bareheaded with his hat in his hand in the gray half-light. She recognized him as the man she had seen from the top of the ridge on her way from the Thorvaldsons'.

He was tall and rangy, and dressed in the conventional "camp" outfit of the outsider: breeches and leggings, brown shirt open at the throat, mackinaw and

slouch hat.   When Lind saw him approaching she smiled
faintly at his ostentatiously appropriate clothes.   She
knew immediately that he was Klovacz's "hired man."

As they passed each other, they exchanged the furtive
survey of strangers meeting in lonely parts.   Lind saw
that he was rugged and brown, with an odd over-casting
of paleness, delicateness; that his eyes were thoughtful
and well set.   Mark Jordan saw only that here was a
girl who was riding in the rain as if she was enjoying it.

Then they passed on.

But Lind could not continue.   She was overcome with
a desire to turn back and stop in at the Klovacz place,
to make some pretext.   He was not an ordinary laborer,
after all.   She held the horse on the road for fully a
minute trying to decide on what to do.   Then it began
to rain in earnest.

The little "sod" house of the Klovaczs, and the few
straggling out-buildings that the recent settlers had
erected, stood in the downpour like huddling outcast
things.   Until two weeks ago this place had been home—
a place to come to from the field, from the bush, from
school.   Lind's eyes grew misty as she thought of the
Klovaczs, that plucky Hungarian family.

The pony trotted up to the "stoop" before the house,
and Lind in a moment was knocking at the door.

Mark Jordan opened it.

"May I come in out of the wet?" Lind smiled, winking
the rain off her eyelashes.   "I am Lind Archer, the
teacher at Oeland."

Mark stepped back and threw the door wider, check-
ing the exclamation that came to his lips.   His keen eye

took in his unexpected guest in a quick sweep, and left him a bit bewildered.

"Hello!" he said. "You're out in bad weather, I'd say. Come right in!"

Lind looked hesitatingly toward the pony, and Mark stepped quickly out of the door. "I'll tend to the horse, Miss Archer. You go in and make yourself comfortable." Standing on the narrow stoop, they looked at each other for a moment rather awkwardly, and then for no reason whatever, both laughed outright. Mark turned away to the pony and Lind went indoors.

She looked about the kitchen into which she had stepped. It already bore that masculine orderliness, where bits of rubbish were brushed out of the way and invisible unless one stooped and looked under stove or cupboard.

Something was cooking on the stove. The oilcloth-covered table was set for one. The rain pattered with myriad fingertips on the pane. Lind pulled down the blind.

Mark Jordan came back into the house. The rain clustered in his dark hair like beads and streamed down his cheeks.

"It's a bad night to be out in," he offered by way of conversation, and then remembered that he had said something like that before. To tell the truth, the coming of Lind when he had given himself up to friendless solitude for an indefinite period had somewhat disconcerted him.

"Oh, I love it," said Lind, happy and at ease. "I love riding or walking in the rain. If you turn me out

I won't be a bit concerned." She laughed up at him from the chair she had taken near the stove.

"Then why did you come at all?" he countered, regaining himself.

"Why—oh, I don't know. I was lonely, I guess," Lind said slowly. "You looked like a human being out there on the road, and I haven't seen a real one for over a month."

"H–m. Well, I hope you won't be disappointed," Mark smiled. Lind saw that he had good white teeth, and a very attractive mouth. "I was just making a little supper. A hermit doesn't eat much for the reason that it's a lot of fuss preparing food for one person. Nearly always make too much or too little."

He had put his foot up on one of the kitchen chairs in front of the fire, and rested his elbow on his knee, while he watched the coffee come to a boil on the stove. Lind removed her soft hat and her jacket. She wore corduroy knickerbockers that were almost waterproof, and stout shoes.

"This is really a cozy little house," she observed.

"Yes," said Mark, glancing about it with her, "not bad at all considering what Klovacz had to go on. Poor devil. I don't expect to see him come back at all." He reached across the stove to a row of pans that hung behind it and took down a small skillet. This he placed on the open fire, dropping into it a spoonful of lard from a can. The lard began to snap and smoke, and he deftly broke two eggs into the skillet. Lind watched him as though she had known him for a long time. He turned toward her.

"Will you set in with me, as they say hereabouts, Miss Archer?" he asked. "Or have you a dinner engagement?"

Lind laughed and said, "Well, if you'll let me do the dishes afterward. I'm afraid there won't be anything left when I get home now, anyway, and Mr Gare doesn't approve of feeding the tardy." She watched Mark comfortably while he went about setting the food on the table. His hands were fine and capable. Lind wondered about him, but asked no questions.

When everything was ready, Mark beckoned her to come to the table. He saw for the first time that she had taken off her hat, and that her hair glowed, smooth and lucent, away from her flushed cheeks. She moved to the chair at the table across from him. They looked at each other. Mark felt suddenly that he could not take his eyes off her.

He pushed his chair back and squatted forward, leaning toward her. His eyes were dark and intent, with a regard that was almost impersonal. Damn it, he thought, it wasn't fair for anyone so lovely to come and take a man unawares!

"I wonder where you came from just now?" he asked curiously.

Lind returned his gaze without smiling. For a moment she seemed to be in a spell of abstraction, unable to answer. Fine whips of rain lashed about the little house, and the wind whistled in the birch trees outside, bleak as a lost bird. These sounds defined the feeling of enclosed warmth and safety in the kitchen of the Klovaczs'. But they did also the opposed thing.

They stirred the fear of loneliness, the ancient dread of abandonment in the wilderness in the profounder natures of these two who found shelter here. For an imponderable moment they sought beyond each other's eyes, sought for understanding, for communion under the vast terrestrial influence that bound them, an inevitable part and form of the earth, inseparable one from the other. The moment was like a warm handclasp.

Lind's eyes dropped to the table. She lifted a fork, and put it down precisely in the same place. Mark Jordan sat with his chin resting on his hand, watching her.

"Down," said Lind, pointing upward with her finger.

"I believe it," he replied seriously. "I think I shall love you."

Lind laughed nervously. He frightened her, with his intent look. He had said that almost as if he wanted to hear how it would sound.

"Do you? Will you tell me what your name is, first?" she said in a light tone, so that she might keep her voice casual. She picked up her fork.

Mark was suddenly astounded at himself. Whatever had come over him to-night? He had probably driven her away.

"Forgive me—I didn't mean to startle you. But I'm quite sure of it. I want you to know that no one ever came to me as you have to-night—as if it were fated. I've been God-forsakenly lonely."

A wave of incredible feeling came over Lind as he spoke. Her impulse was to rush over to him and touch this strange man's hair, run her fingers through it so that he should no longer be a stranger to her.

"Oh!" she cried, "I know that—so well!" She stretched her hand out suddenly on the table and leaned toward him. He put his own over it with a light pressure, and they smiled at each other.

"But you haven't yet told me your name?" she reminded him.

He straightened in his chair. "Oh, lord no—I haven't! It's Jordan—Mark Jordan. Now let's eat. You must be hungry." He passed her the bread.

"How's the coffee?" he asked brusquely after a moment.

"Very, *very* good," she assured him. "I think you're a surprisingly good cook."

The tension was for the moment broken, and they seemed to become fast friends in a few minutes. So they ate together, eggs and fried potatoes, bread and preserved wild plums that the Klovaczs had left, and coffee. They talked of the life at Oeland and of the harsh charm of it that each had felt upon arrival. Mark had not yet had time to get acquainted with the settlers. Lind sketched them to him in brief, sharp outlines. He was amused by her observations.

"The Sandbos are your nearest neighbors," she informed him. "Mrs Sandbo thinks she is happy in the death of her husband, but in reality he is more alive now than he ever was."

She told him of the Gares and the leaden spell that seemed to hang over them all.

"Judith is a beautiful creature. She's like a—a wild horse, more than anything I know of. But Caleb doesn't give her a moment to herself even to think in. I seldom get near her, much as I should like to know her better."

"Hm—you could do a lot for the girl, I should think, if you got the chance," said Mark.

He told her a little of himself, of his upbringing among the priests in whose care he had been left upon the death of his father, whom he did not remember; the little he knew of his mother, an English gentlewoman who had died while he was still an infant; of his profession, and his hope of returning to the city at the end of six months with renewed eagerness to work. And Lind in turn told him of how she had happened to come here, and of her resolve to stay in spite of the rancor of Caleb Gare and the terrible oppression in his household.

Lind finally whisked the dishes off the table and washed them, while Mark dried and set them in a neat row in the cupboard. Then Lind looked out the window and observed that the rain had nearly stopped.

"Mrs Gare will think I am at the Sandbos', and will not worry. But I must be getting home," she said. Mark took his cap and coat off the wall and they went out together. There was still a thin rain and the trees were great watery blots against the darkening sky.

Mark fed and watered Lind's pony, then saddled a horse for himself. Lind stood in the dark stable while he got ready. There was a snug intimacy about the low-ceilinged log barn with the drip of the rain faintly audible on the roof, that made her doubly aware of Mark's nearness.

He did not bother to light a lantern for the saddling of his horse. He worked hastily in the darkness lest the feeling he had toward this unaccountable girl should sweep him off his feet completely. When he was ready he walked the horse out, brushing against Lind who did not at once see him. The brief contact made his heart beat unreasonably.

With the sensitive rain on their faces, they rode down the wood trail, the horses side by side.

Although he had intended turning back long before, Mark rode with Lind well over the miles that led to the Gare farm. The rain stopped and finally overhead a great billow of hurrying cloud broke and revealed a misty star. From the northern swamps came a solitary hollow call, as if it was blown by a wind. It was the honking of a belated wild goose, the last to fly over the land to the half frozen marshes of the remoter north. Lind and Mark listened, standing still, then looked at each other. Suddenly, it seemed, the air had cleared, and the night stood over them, wide, infinite, transparent as a strange dream. . . .

2

Amelia was getting a pail of water from the well when Lind returned.

"Have you had supper, Miss Archer?" she asked as Lind came up to her. There was an almost anxious note in Amelia's voice.

"Yes, thanks, I have," Lind replied rather breathlessly.

She was flushed and preoccupied after taking leave of Mark Jordan.

Amelia looked after her keenly. Lind turned suddenly and came back to give the woman a hand with the pail.

"I've had an adventure to-night, Mrs Gare," Lind confided. "I've been riding with a most interesting man, and a handsome one, too."

Amelia smiled. She thought Lind was joking. "Who is he? He must have dropped down with the rain."

"He is Klovacz's hired man—just for a while. Out here for his health, or his nerves, rather. He's not a farm hand by nature, of course," Lind told her, and then could have bitten her tongue through for her thoughtless words. Intuitively she felt Amelia wince.

"What is his name?"

"Oh, what is it, anyway? Jordan—Mark Jordan," Lind said.

"Wh–what?"

"Mark Jordan," Lind repeated, pulling at the pail which seemed suddenly to have thrown all its weight into her hand. Amelia paused for a moment as if she were staring at something in the dark pasture beyond the fence.

"What is it?" Lind asked, looking in the same direction.

For a moment Amelia stood dumb. Her hand on the pail was limp.

"Do you see anything, Mrs Gare?" Lind urged, glancing at her.

The woman's face in the indefinite light was expressionless, stony. When Lind spoke the second time, she started, and jerked at the handle of the pail.

"No—no . . . I thought I saw something. Bears around," she murmured. "Martin must tend to those sheep pens."

They went indoors and Lind released the pail.

Caleb was reading his weekly agriculture journal in the light of the lamp in the sitting room. After she had removed her outer clothing Lind came and sat at the table also, laying out her work for the morrow. Caleb did not glance up or speak to her. Lind had the feeling that he disapproved of her being absent from meals. She smiled to herself.

Amelia entered the room and changed the chimney of the lamp, polishing the one she had taken off with a woolen cloth. During the momentary flickering of the light Caleb hitched his shoulders impatiently.

Amelia spoke to Caleb lightly about the good amount of rain that had fallen, and casually mentioned the fact that she would soon have to be sending to the "mail order" for garden seed. Caleb made no response but shifted his position finally so that his back was almost directly toward her. Amelia smiled at the Teacher, almost mischievously. Lind had never seen her in this lively, self-possessed mood. She wondered what had caused it.

The others, after an unusually heavy day, had gone to bed early. In a little while Lind also went up to the loft. Caleb and Amelia were left alone.

"You didn't tell me he had come here," Amelia darted out. Her eyes shone above white cheeks. She stood at the side of the table and began with both hands to roll up the edge of the table cloth into a tight little furl.

Caleb turned slowly. "Heh!" he sneered. "You found out, didn't you?"

"Yes, I found out," Amelia repeated, holding each word as if she were trying to memorize it. "The Teacher has talked to him."

Caleb raised his eyebrows, and drew his left hand across his mustache. So the Teacher had done her little part, had she? He might have known that soft eyed chit would not keep her place.

"Well? Are you going to fall on his neck? He'll thank ye for it," he said. He turned the pages of the journal, and Amelia heard his short clucking laugh. Her hands tightened on the rolled cloth.

"No . . . I won't do anything," she said.

Caleb got up, looked into the stove, spat into it, and started to take off his shoes.

Without another remark he went to bed.

For the first time in his life, it was uncertainty that kept him silent, not the confidence that his will was understood without the utterance of his word.

CHAPTER V

1

ANTON KLOVACZ had left a five acre plot of scrub brush for Mark Jordan to clear. On the day after Lind's visit he began "slashing," going down into the bush with his ax after he had tended to the animals. The air was cool and clear, admirable for hard labor. He swung the ax with rapid, clean sweeps, enjoying the feel of the smooth wood handle on his palms.

He thought of Lind Archer. Late the night before he had lain awake thinking of her. She had made him feel for the first time in his life that he was not hopelessly locked within himself. Her physical radiance alone carried him beyond himself, but that might have been simply explained away since she was the only woman he had seen or was likely to see during his sojourn here. Unreasonable and out of keeping with his conceptions as it seemed, the deepest pulse of his being had leaped in recognition of her as he had looked across the table into her eyes the night before. The whole circumstance made him feel very humble and diffident now as he reviewed it. He must see her again, at once, and yet he feared to meet her lest he should disclose his feelings and find them unwelcome to her. And yet, he could not persuade himself that she had not responded to him in part, at least. He knew his own impetuous, strong desires so well, and he realized that to see much of Lind here would be a torment to him, especially if he should learn, for instance,

that there was some one else in her life. He would have
to see her again.in a day or two, call at the school perhaps, and ask permission to see her at the Gares. That
would be the proper procedure. The modest country
swain courting . . . he grinned as he thought of himself
in the new rôle. And yet how different life seemed to-day.
He rested one hand on the end of the ax and loosened
his shirt about the throat. His eyes drifted down the
stretch of Klovacz's land where the homesteader's elder
sons had planted fodder grains before their departure.
The landscape seemed to have a gentler look than it had
yesterday.

Lind . . . Lind Archer—what a pretty name it was!
There had never been any one so suddenly complete, so
gratifying to the complex and dubious thing that was
himself—the self that had come out of nowhere and had
always seemed to belong nowhere in spite of his advan-
tages of education and natural endowment. Mark
found himself wanting her again beside him, wanting
her terribly as some one from whom he had never in his
life been separated.

He struggled to reason with himself. He had no
right to dream about her this way. The next time he
saw her he would keep himself well in check. He began
again energetically slashing the ranks of choked birch
trees right and left.

2

Fusi Aronson, on foot, came to deal with Caleb Gare
in regard to a bit of timber land. He came with great

strides across the country, like some giant defender of a forgotten race.

To fortify himself against killing Caleb Gare outright, he stopped to talk with the Teacher in her school.

"I would do it now, but you say it would be no good. That is true: somehow his time will come," Fusi agreed.

He shook hands with Lind soberly and she admonished him once more against using violence on Caleb. Fusi, the great Icelander, proceeded across the road to make a sale of a certain piece of wood land.

3

Days flow on, even after the coming of an event of great purport. Even after great sorrow and great gladness, days flow on, and all things become the shining woof and the shadowed warp of the tapestry of the past. So went the day of Lind's finding Mark Jordan, and Amelia's learning of it.

The Teacher came into the house after school on the day following the rain, to find Amelia bending over a half-completed piece-quilt which she had stretched out on the floor. She kept her eyes lowered to the bright squares and triangles of the quilt. A bar of sunlight, falling from the window across her sandy hair, cut the quilt diagonally.

"What a gay comforter that's going to be!" Lind exclaimed, stooping to touch a bit of yellow satin. "How long did it take you to collect enough pieces?"

Amelia did not answer at once, and when she did it was without raising her eyes. Lind divined that she had been crying. Her impulse was to kneel beside Amelia and ask her what the trouble was, but she had come in a short time to know that sympathy would only embarrass her. Whatever her grief, she jealously kept it to herself as if it were too intimate for unburdening. The gaudy pieces of the quilt shimmered and blazed.

"These are odds and ends I've been saving since the twins were born," Amelia said at last. "We don't have much use for silks here you know. I thought I'd save up until the girls grew old enough to appreciate a nice cover."

Lind knelt and fingered one of the larger pieces of silk. "That's pretty—a kind of brocade, isn't it? Was it a dress?"

"Yes—one that I had a long time before I was married."

"It must have been beautiful."

Amelia made no reply, and Lind, with a dozen fancies about the dress and where and how it had been worn, got to her feet and went out of doors. Before what was called the front of the log house, Ellen was planting sweet peas under a window.

"There must be something—something over-ruling—greater than life, even," Lind thought about Amelia.

Ellen looked up, blinking.

"Oh, I thought you were mother," she laughed as Lind stopped beside her. "This light gets me all mixed up."

Lind knew it was not the light.

"Ellen, when are you going to get new glasses?"

Ellen glanced down at the flower bed.

"Oh, these will do till the doctor comes to the Siding again."

Lind knew that they had already done too long—perhaps forever too long.

"Ellen," began Lind, squatting on the ground beside the girl. "Would your father let me buy glasses for you?"

"Oh, dear, don't say anything like that to him!" Ellen cried. "He intends to get them for me—only he forgets. It isn't the money."

Ellen's discomfort was so apparent that Lind could say nothing more. Her defense of her father was a pitiful thing. There was nothing she could do—no help she could give that would be accepted. Even Judith was proud and distant when it came to gifts. She would not take Lind's amber beads, for instance—insisted that they did not become her at all.

"Ellen, are you going to stay here all your life?" Lind asked quietly.

Ellen tore a corner off a package of seed and poured some of the contents into her hand.

"What else is there for me to do?" she returned, a slightly hostile line appearing at either side of her mouth. "There's nothing the matter with this place, is there? I've lived here long enough to like it if you don't." Lind had never before heard her speak with such emotion. Her head was thrown back defiantly, her flat cheeks faintly pink.

"Oh, Ellen, you know what I mean! You are bright, intelligent—with a little education you could make a great deal of yourself. You are wasted here. Have you never asked your father to let you go away for a while?"

"No," she answered indifferently. "I don't want to go." Along the little trench she had dug she sifted the seeds.

"Don't tell me that, Ellen," Lind persevered. "You do. I don't want to turn you against your own home, or anything like that, dear. But I see such fine things in you—your love of music, for instance. Your father could afford to do without you for a few months every year, I'm sure. Why don't you ask him?"

"It's no use for you to talk, Miss Archer," Ellen returned calmly. She sometimes called Lind "teacher," but never used her first name. "I know just how hard he has to work to give us this home, and I know he can't do without any of us. It's not for you to say."

Lind got to her feet, hurt in spite of herself at Ellen's attitude. She knew very well that the girl did not really believe what she said. But the contorted sense of loyalty that had been inbred in Ellen had overrun every other instinct like a choking tangle of weeds. She reasoned only as Caleb had taught her to reason, in terms of advantage to the land and to him.

Lind went into the house and got a favorite book of verse which she took with her down the wood road past the school house to a little green mound overlooking a marsh full of marigolds. Here she seated herself and tried to see the words on the page before her. But somehow her eyes would lift and lose themselves in the clear distance, where the long reeds stood like etchings of green and gold in the sun. She found herself wondering about Mark Jordan, and, ridiculously enough con-

necting him with the auguring of the ancient grandmother of the Bjarnassons. She had not invited him to
call on her at the Gares'. It did not seem fitting somehow, although she knew he had wanted her to suggest it.
So there seemed to be nothing for it but to make an errand to the Klovacz place. . . .

With her long, smooth fingers she dug a half black,
half white, stone loose from the earth at her side.

"If the other side is mostly white, old Grandma Bjarnasson's tale is true. If black, not true," she whimsied.
The other side of the little stone was all white. Lind
smiled to herself.

4

Every evening that Jude went for the cattle her eye
roved in the direction of the Sandbos'. Any day now,
Sven would come home. She knew that he would be
looking for her, although he would not venture actually
to the Gare farm. Caleb had, in the past, made it clear
that young Sven Sandbo was not welcome on the place.
His smile and the easy swagger of his shoulders were
a little too impudent.

At sunset one evening in the middle of May, Judith
rode the colt, Turk, north across the grazing land like
some dark young goddess, her hair low against the
horse's mane, her blood avid for speed. She was conscious of the picture she made, magnificently riding.
And she was conscious of being watched. She reined
in suddenly and threw up her head. Her cheeks, already crimson, grew hot with color, her eyelids dropped.

Then, with a sweeping flourish of her whip, she rode forward to meet Sven Sandbo.

Sven was walking across the open stretch between his own home and the brush that belonged to Fusi Aronson on the north. From here one could not be seen by any one at the Gares'. Sven came up to her and rested his arms across the damp neck of the horse.

"You look great, Jude," he said, looking at her deliberately from head to foot. His hand ran over her overalled thigh. She drew her foot back in the stirrup with a jerk. Sven laughed and thrust his hands into his pockets. He threw his weight on one foot and crossed the other lazily in front of it. "How's everything to home?" he asked.

Judith returned his searching glance with equal deliberateness; took in coolly the city cut of his clothes, his flaming tie, his long shining shoes that had no bumps on the toes such as Martin's yellow Sunday shoes had; and she made no comment upon his appearance. She knew that Sven expected her to.

Sven was no fool. He laughed, and when he laughed there was no woman could withstand him, he had found. He had the most engagingly male smile in the world.

"Aw, come on, Jude, you ain't sore on me," he coaxed, shaking her foot. "How are *you,* that's what I'd like to know."

"I'm all right," she replied coldly. "How are *you?*"

"Fine. Couldn't wait till I got back. Thought about you all the time, and I would o' written, too, if I thought the old man wouldn't get hold of it. Gosh, you're prettier 'n ever, Jude. Girls in town can't hold a candle to you. I've seen 'em all."

He whipped out a sterling silver cigarette case and held it so that it flashed in the sun. It seemed that he kept it out unnecessarily long to draw a cigarette from it. Judith looked away to the horizon, and her horse stamped an impatient hoof. Sven put a hand on the horse's bridle, snapped the case together and slipped it back in his pocket.

"Come riding with me some night? I'll rot here if I don't do something—or see somebody," said he, indolently blowing the smoke upward into the air and flipping off the ash of his cigarette with his forefinger. He had not done that before he went away. Do something —see somebody, that was what he wanted to do, was it? Not something or somebody in particular.

Judith sat silent, her eyes moodily on the distance.

"Oh, that reminds me," he went on, "here's something I got you. All the girls are carryin' 'em." He drew a little package out of his pocket and unwrapped it. From the tissue paper he took out a gold plated vanity case which he held up to Judith, looking at her face for the smile of surprise he fully expected to see there.

Judith gave the thing a quick glance.

Then with a swift twist of her body she forced the horse to rear upright on his hind legs, his mouth wide, nostrils distended, eyes swimming. She dropped her head against his mane, wheeled him about and was off in an instant on an animal that had gone mad.

Sven, completely dazed, stared after her, saw the horse

jerk from the road and take the fence that enclosed a hay-field at a fine long sweep, like a slender boat rising on a wave.

"Well—I'll be—" he marveled. "By gosh, she's a live one. Worse'n ever. What did she get sore at, any-way?"

But Sven felt uneasily that he knew. She thought he had been showing off.

Galloping away on the horse, Judith gave way to tears.

5

The days grew steadily warmer and longer, the distance over field and brush took on a deeper green. Caleb's herds on the prairie westward sought shelter from the noonday sun under the trees on the bluffs, and the milch cows in the north pasture gave up nibbling sweet-grass for long moments to stand knee-deep in the tepid swamps already a-drone with insects that ricocheted like sparks across the surface of the water. The season of cold morning dews changed to that of fireflies and evening mist. The yield of the earth passed from timorous seedling to rugged stalk and stem.

But in the life in the Gare household there was no apparent change, no growth or maturing of dreams or fears, no evidence of crises in personal struggle, no peak of achievement rapturously reached. There was no outward emotion or expressed thought save that which led as a great tributary to the flow of Caleb's ambition. He talked now day and night of nothing but the livestock, circled the fields by day in the cart or walked abroad with his lantern alone at night, and compared the strength of his hay and his flax with that of Skuli Erickson or Joel Brund, the husband of Mrs Sandbo's daughter Dora. The early summer season was to him a terrific, prolonged hour of passion during which he was blind and deaf and dumb to everything save the impulse that bound him to the land.

His flax was growing in such a way that he scarcely dared look at it lest it should vanish like a vision. He would put off examining it for a week at a time for fear that in a twinkling something dire had happened to it.

But smoothly as affairs seemed to run on the surface of life at the Gares', there had been a subtle diverting of the undercurrent. Lind Archer perceived it and was troubled.

Sven Sandbo had come home. And Judith's behavior was incomprehensible. Lind had tried to talk to her about him, but she had walked rudely away. And when Lind had offered Judith a book to read which had been sent her from the city, the girl's manner had been much more like Ellen's than her own. She had no time for the book, she had said. Amelia was preoccupied these days, and her attitude toward Caleb had become almost one of indulgence. There had been a letting down of the familiar tension on Amelia's part, and a tightening of restraint on the part of Judith. Caleb for a time was too engrossed in the affairs of the farm to notice any one. Unlike himself, he went puttering about haphazard trifles, constantly looking for something to do rather than, as usual, for something that Martin or Judith might do.

Lind felt that something momentous had happened, and then realized how impossible it was for anything at all to happen here save the monotonous round of duty.

It was Lind alone who noticed these nuances in the life at the Gares. She had much time to herself in the evenings when she sat at her desk after the children were gone, and fell often to thinking about the Gares. But since the evening of the rain she had thought more of Mark Jordan.

On the third day after her visit at the Klovacz place, Lind sat at her desk in the school house. The children had been dismissed. The room was heavy with the smell of chalk and plum blossoms. Lind felt tired and rather depressed. She closed her eyes and leaned her head against the palms of her hands. She went in detail again over the frightening and delicious night of the rain.

The door opened slowly. Mark Jordan stood framed against the light, smiling, bareheaded, his hat in his hand. Lind clapped her hands to her cheeks. Then she laughed.

"You look guilty," said Mark. He came slowly down the aisle in the center of the room, looking at her happily.

"I confess I am," Lind said shyly. "I was thinking of inviting myself to dinner again at your house." She got up from her desk and stretched her hand out to him. He held it, looked at it, pointed to the chalk and ink stains.

"Salt of the earth: a school teacher. I was one myself for about a month. Got fired for encouraging the kids to play hookey," he laughed. He dropped her hand and strode around the room examining the drawings and knick-knacks the children had made and hung on the walls. Taking a piece of chalk he drew on the blackboard a ridiculous figure with knock-knees and turned-in eyes, and under it wrote in a childish scrawl. "Teacher." Then he stepped back ten paces and took aim with the chalk, succeeding in tossing it on the ledge of the blackboard. This he did several times, stepping back a few paces farther each time.

Lind watched the game for a while half-amusedly. Then she was conscious of a faint irritation. He apparently had forgotten she was there. His restlessness shut her out. Irrelevantly she recalled the words of the ancient grandmother of the Bjarnassons: she would never know the secret of him. As he stood in profile to her, her eyes outlined the well-bred shape of his head and shoulders. He turned to her so suddenly that she started.

"Let's walk," he said. "What's the matter?"

"Nothing," she answered. She would have to try to understand him. "I really don't want to walk now that you have decided upon it for me so peremptorily. But I'll use you as a means to control my temper, and go with you. You are terribly used to having your own way, I can see that. As if you were the only person on earth."

"I always was—until you came, Lind. I just have to get used to the idea of your presence," he said, so seriously that she had to smile.

"Did any of the Gares see you come in here?" she asked uneasily.

"The Gares? Oh, those people? Don't know. I didn't see anybody except a robin in the road, and he didn't even turn a feather," he told her, going to the window while she cleared her desk. "Why? Are you afraid of them?"

"Oh, by no means," she said hastily. "It's just that I don't want them to—oh, I want to know you separately from them—in another world, so to speak. If you go there, or talk with them, I'll feel that the *idea* of you has mingled with them. See? I don't want you to see them or them to see you, except, perhaps, Judith—" She glanced at him thoughtfully, as if to make up her mind as to the good judgment that lay in the reservation.

"You walked?" she asked, after they had slipped out and had taken a little path that insinuated itself through the thick growth of fir trees behind the school house.

"No, I came on an elephant. It evaporated at your door," he said, and they both laughed.

"But curiosity impels me to see this Gare family," Mark declared a little later. "Especially Caleb Gare. They told me at Yellow Post that he's the devil himself."

"No, he's too cowardly to be the devil. He's too cowardly even for a man to want to kill him. That's why Fusi Aronson hasn't done it long ago."

She told him about Fusi.

"I'd like to meet him," Mark said.

They talked of the strange unity between the nature of man and earth here in the north, and of the spareness of both physical and spiritual life.

"There's no waste—that's it," Mark observed, "either in human relationships or in plant growth. There's no incontinency anywhere. I've made trips around Yellow

Post since I've been here, and I haven't talked with a single farmer who wasn't looking forward to the time when he wouldn't have a grain of any kind in his bins if he didn't rake and scrape for all he's worth now. They seem to have no confidence in the soil—no confidence in anything save their own labor. Think of the difference there would be in the outward characters of these people if the land didn't sap up all their passion and sentiment."

Lind nodded. "That's what's wrong with the Gares. They all have a monstrously exaggerated conception of their duty to the land—or rather to Caleb, who is nothing but a symbol of the land."

They sat down upon a flat rock near the trail.

"I spent some time farther north—went up to a mission when I was only a kid with one of the priests, and later after I had grown up," Mark told her. "That's a country for you. If there's a God, I imagine that's where he sits and does his thinking. The silence is awful. You feel immense things going on, invisibly. There is that eternal sky—light and darkness—the endless plains of snow—a few fir-trees, maybe a hill or a frozen stream. And the human beings are like totems—figures of wood with mysterious legends upon them that you can never make out. The austerity of nature reduces the outward expression in life, simply, I think, because there is not such an abundance of natural objects for the spirit to react to. We are, after all, only the mirror of our environment. Life here at Oeland, even, may seem a negation but it's only a reflection from so few exterior natural objects that it has the semblance of negation. These people are thrown inward upon themselves, their passions stored up, they are intensified figures of life with no outward expression—no releasing gesture."

"Yes, I think perhaps human life, or at least human contact, is just as barren here as farther north," Lind remarked. "The struggle against conditions must have the same effect as passivity would have, ultimately. It seems to me that one would be as dulling as the other— one would extort as much from human capacity for expression as the other. There's no feeling left after the soil and the live stock have taken their share."

They talked about books and disagreed spiritedly here and there. Mark urged her to let him come to see her at the Gares' and bring with him two or three of his treasured volumes, and she consented to speak to Mrs Gare about it.

To Lind it was miraculous that she should have found him here. To Mark it seemed the most natural thing in the world that he should have found her.

"I may come to the school house then any evening?" Mark asked almost timidly. It was time for him to go, and it amazed him that he hated so to leave her. She put out her hand to him simply.

"Yes, do," she said warmly. They had come within sight of the gate at the Gares'.

He looked at her oddly, then turned and walked rapidly down the road. He looked back once, and saw her standing where he had left her. Raising his slouch hat he waved his arm in a wide arc. Lind walked on into

the barnyard of the Gares'. Her heart was beating bois-
terously.

6

Shearing time was at hand. Thirty-odd sheep, so heavily coated that they looked clumsy in their own wool,
were herded into the pen where Judith, Martin, Amelia
and Ellen proceeded with the work of shearing. The
smell of the wool always nauseated Ellen, so Amelia
contrived to have her indoors with the housework a large
part of the time. Judith moved among the sheep, sin-
gling out her own to see that justice was done in regard
to the disposition of the wool. It had been a point with
Caleb since the children were little to let them have a few
animals of their own to bring up and sell, and in this manner pay for their own clothing. He contended that it
gave them an active interest in the business of the farm
and instilled in them early a feeling of independence.
Amelia had long since seen through this mock generosity.

Caleb, although he did not materially assist in the
task, paused before the pen where the three were at work,
after Ellen had gone indoors. Beside him stood Thorvald Thorvaldson, the Icelander, who prided himself
upon being a Master. Caleb rested his elbows on the
board fence and gave arbitrary instructions in regard to
the shearing. It gave him the gratifying feeling of over-
seer.

"Here, Jude! That's no way to clip! Get the shears
under it more—come along! Come along! Can't take

all day with a sheep, you know. Little closer there!
Fine wool, eh, Thorvald? How many pounds do you
reckon I'll get off that sheep?"

Judith turned her back directly on the two men and
kept at her work. The sheep was one of her pets, a ewe
who always bore well. Judith hated the Icelander, who
stood glowering above her. She had glanced sideways up
at him and had found his piggish little eyes surveying
her limbs and the backs of her thighs as she bent over,
the overalls she wore tightening across her body. She
dug down into the ewe's chest and clenched a fistful of
the thick wool. There were limits to endurance, even
for Amelia's sake.

Amelia did not glance up. Her serenity troubled
Caleb. It was a change in her he could not fathom. It
had come with her discovery that Mark Jordan was on
the Klovacz homestead. You could never rely on how
any woman would react to a thing, not even Amelia.

"Come, come, Amelia! Thorvald is thirsty. Plenty
of time to finish that before dark," he said to her. His
tone was like a sudden prod in the back. Amelia
straightened quickly, brushed a wisp of dun colored hair
out of her eyes. The homely gesture gave her an uncouth look for an instant, a pitiful gaucheness.

"I thought you said Mr Thorvaldson had no time for
coffee?"

Caleb stared at her. "Mr Thorvaldson will have coffee. He has changed his mind," he said finally, turning
with the glum-faced, inscrutable Icelander to the house.
No mention of coffee had been made to Thorvaldson.
He grinned flatteringly at Caleb. Here indeed was con-

trol that was at once subtle and sure! The trouble was that Thorvaldson's women folk had not the intelligence to understand and properly respect such ruling. More obvious tactics had to be used with them. . . .

"How is your wife coming?" Amelia asked Thorvald when she had served him with coffee.

"She's coming long purty good," he responded, emptying the contents of his saucer down his throat. "Coming in soon, I t'ink, haa! haa! Vun after another—such a voman!"

Amelia turned away from the man. He had grotesque, overhanging mustaches that trailed in the saucer he held to his mouth. Caleb was filling his pipe. He saw Amelia turn away. He saw the tightening about her lips.

Caleb smiled cunningly. "Sit down, my dear," he said, placing a chair for her directly in front of Thorvald. "The shearing can wait. Have a chat with Thorvald. Heh, heh! My wife gets sick of seein' only her husband around, Thorvaldson. A woman should have a change, eh?" Both men laughed heartily, Caleb tilting back his head and letting his eyes rest casually on Amelia, who had without a word sat down into the chair he indicated.

Amelia's eyes wandered to the window. They were not timid, submissive, as they had been a week ago. They were nervous, alert. Caleb was disturbed.

Thorvald swallowed great fistfuls of bread and butter and cold meat that Amelia had set out for him, swallowed with an eager noise. Amelia sat before him, uttering not a word.

Yes, Caleb was disturbed. He made up his mind once more that Amelia must not set eyes on Mark Jordan.

After the departure of Thorvald Thorvaldson, Caleb approached his wife. His voice was smooth, easy.

"The Teacher has talked with that son of yours again. If she asks to have him come here, remember it isn't best. For one thing, Amelia, it would only remind you of things you want to forget. For another, he's not the kind I want to have round my children." He lit his pipe again leisurely, as if he had spoken of the most commonplace of things, and went out the door scarcely lifting his feet off the ground, his head thrust forward, his hands clasped behind him. He had been satisfied with Amelia's pallor. Whatever her state of mind, he must assure himself that he could in a moment change it. That was control.

7

The shearing completed, and the wool packed into flour sacks ready to be taken to the Siding of Nykerk, the round of more usual work began again.

While Ellen worked in the vegetable garden, weeding and hoeing, until her narrow back was numb from the strain, Judith made a number of trips to Yellow Post in the dog cart for provisions.

"Yes!" she burst out at Ellen who finally reproached her for her selfishness. "Why do you stick? I'm not sorry for you. I'm not sorry for any of us! We're all old enough to get out. Why do you stick, if you don't like it? I don't like it and I'm going to get out—soon. I'm not going through another winter up to my knees in manure—not much! I've handled enough calves for him! What do I get for it? What do you get for it?

It was different when we were small and she couldn't help herself. I tell you—I'm quitting!" Her voice rose to an uncontrollable pitch, her full breasts shook.

Ellen adjusted her glasses over her nose, a thing she always did when under excitement of any kind.

"Judith," she said solemnly. "It isn't only that. There's something else. He has some kind of threat he always makes to her—you've heard him—I've heard him. I don't know what it is, but she's afraid—afraid of what he'll do. We can't let him do it. You know we can't. It would kill her. I have given up a lot more than you ever will to stay——"

"Oh . . ." Judith gave vent to a word that made Ellen start.

"Judith, you're dreadful!"

"I'm worse than you think! A lot worse!" said Jude, driving off in the cart.

Lind was awaiting her at the school house.

"You look angry, Judie, what's the matter now?" Lind asked her when they were on their way.

"Nothing, but Ellen makes me sick with her whining. She loves to suffer. And loves to see everybody else doing it. But just because she isn't quite as strong as I am she gets it only half as bad."

"I don't think she loves it at all, Judie. I think she is giving up a great deal to stay on here, and she knows it. Has there ever been anybody that she cared for very much—who wanted to marry her?"

"I guess old Goat-eyes liked her all right. But he's been gone a year, and she never talks about him. Anyway, he's a halfbreed, or nearly."

"Of course, if Ellen loved him, that wouldn't have mattered, do you think?"

"No, I s'pose not.   He was too good for her, anyway."
Judith's eyes were full of intolerant contempt.   She
slapped the horse's rump with the reins, and the rattle of
the cart soon made conversation difficult.   They did not
stop at Sandbos', as Jude knew that Caleb would be spying from the slight rise on which the Gare farm was built
to see that the horse emerged from around the bend in
due time.

Yellow Post lay in a little valley shaped like the palm
of a hand, a narrow creek curving across it like a life
line.   Jude drove briskly up to the store of Johanneson,
the Swede trader, and Lind went into the store to make a
few purchases of her own while Judith tied up the horse.
A few halfbreeds ventured into the store after her, to
skulk about with furtive glances.

Leaning against the counter in the store and smoking
his pipe, stood Mark Jordan.   He came toward her with
a quick stride, looking down at her almost querulously.

"You didn't come," he said in a low tone, glancing with
annoyance at the open stares about them.

"Come—where—when?" Lind asked innocently.

"Let's go outside and talk," he said.   He picked up his
box of groceries and steered Lind out of the door before
she had an opportunity to make her own purchases.
Judith passed them at the doorway.

"Come on out after you've got your things, Judie,"
Lind called back to her.   The girl went on into the store,
showing none of the curiosity she felt about the stranger
who was with Lind.

Mark placed his provisions in the bottom of the buggy in which he had driven to Yellow Post, and walked with Lind to the creek. They sat down on the grassy bank and watched the tiny minnows dart down with the gentle current in silver schools, and turning, snub their way quiveringly back up stream with no more provocation, perhaps, than the shadow of a sailing leaf on the water.

"I've missed you. It rained last night, and I was sure you'd come," Mark told her. "I listened until midnight."

"Oh, how ridiculous! You did not!"

"I swear it!"

"But it would be a little—irregular."

Mark frowned at her. "It wasn't the night you did come. You do the thing you want to here, anyway. I need you, Lind, more than you know. I've been plugging away clearing Klovacz's land, or I would have been over at the school yesterday. Has Mrs Gare given you permission to have me call on you?"

"I've not asked her yet. It's terribly hard. But I'll come over and cook you a dinner—" she said impulsively. "May I bring Judith? That's Jude back in the store."

Mark gave her a searching look.

"Oh, just to make it jollier," she hastened to add.

"Bring her, by all means, and any one else you like."

They walked back toward the store. As Jude did not come out, Lind decided that she felt shy about meeting Mark, and did not go in for her. She said good-by to him, and Mark climbed into the buggy and drove off.

It was the day on which mail arrived with John To-bacco, and when Lind returned alone to the store, Sven

Sandbo was there talking with Judith. Sven had discarded his city clothes and most of his braggadocio air. His heavy shoulders stood out from his narrow hips, the calves of his legs were slightly bowed from the saddle. The mobility of his mouth and nostrils, the lazy droop of his eyes at the corners, the careless gesture of the hand that held his cigarette, his frank maleness, made him at once attractive and exasperating.

Judith, hostile-eyed and withdrawn, was trying hard not to smile at his advances.

"Tell me," he was saying, "do you like me better with-out my tenderfoot get-up?"

"A little," she admitted. "But you think you're too smart."

Sven laughed teasingly. "Wouldn't notice my clothes the other day at all, would you? And me comin' all the way from town just to show you 'em. You hurt my feelin's, Jude, terrible!" She looked sternly away and he moved closer to her. "Have you forgot all about the picnic last summer, Judie? Remember what you said? I ain't forgot." His voice was so low that the pitch of it alone made Judith blush.

Lind, followed by the nudges and leering eyes of the halfbreeds who hung about, came up to Jude, who introduced her to Sven. Sven, quite at ease, talked with the Teacher while Judith argued with Johanneson over the merits of a certain dried codfish.

"What's the matter?" Johanneson demanded. "That's good fish, and double worth the money. Guess yer paw give ye only ten cents to buy for, ha?"

Judith tossed her head angrily. "You keep still, you

flat-faced Swede! If there was another store here we'd not give our good money for your bum stuff. Give me a dollar's worth of the fish, and be quick about it!" She stamped her foot and all the men in the store looked toward her appreciatively. She had been told to get only fifty cents worth of the fish. She would have to explain to Amelia, who would understand well enough, but perhaps not approve.

Johanneson turned sheepishly about and wrapped up the package of cod. He could not afford, on second thought, to lose Gare as a customer. But this big girl's insolent quibbling over prices always annoyed him. No doubt she had been prompted by those at home.

Still somewhat ruffled, Judith went out with Sven, followed immediately by Lind when she had made her purchases. The two girls got into their own cart and Sven drove slowly away alone behind them.

"Lind," said Judith, when they were out of sight of Yellow Post, "Sven asked me to ride with him. Will you take the cart home? And I'll get out and wait for him."

"But your father——"

"I don't care. I get hell anyway."

Lind obligingly, though with some misgivings, took the cart home, and Judith rode with Sven.

"Judie," Sven began, putting an arm around her shoulders. "I want you to marry me."

Judith was silent. She thought of Amelia. Ellen would never forgive her. . . .

"Don't you love me any more, Judie? You used to," said Sven, almost humbly.

Judith's head was high, her eyes half-closed. The buggy rumbled down the hollow over a little bridge that led through a dense growth of spruce and cedar. Sven drew her suddenly into his arms, letting the reins fall slack over his knees.

"Damn—you're beautiful, Judie!"

Judith smiled. Her body softened toward him. It rippled with strength. She was peculiarly aware of her strength. It seemed to flow upward from her spine in a powerful current and issue from her breast and her fingertips and all the sensitive surface of her body. A strange desire seized her. She could not free herself from the obsession . . . it had come upon her first the day she had seen Sven after his return.

"I wonder if I can throw you," she said suddenly.

Sven laughed aloud.

"I'll bet I can," she asserted. "Let me try."

"All right, some time," he agreed, laughing still.

"No, right now," Judith insisted, her eyes roving over the muscles that moved under his shirt sleeve.

It was warm and neither wore a coat.

Sven glanced at her and saw that she was in earnest. They got down from the buggy, tying the horse to a tree at the side of the road. Then they crawled through the fence into a little clearing among the cedars, where the sunlight lay in a warm pool on the ground.

"Kiss me first," said Sven.

"No—after," Judith said steadily.

So they wrestled. Judith was almost as tall as Sven. Her limbs were long, sinewy, her body quick and lithe as a wild-cat's. Sven, who started the tussle laughing, could get no lasting grip on her. She slid through his arms and wound herself about his body, bringing them both to the earth. As their movements increased in swiftness and strength, Sven forgot to laugh and became as serious as Judith. It did not occur to him that he might have to use his real energy in defending himself until he saw that the girl's face was set and hard, her eyes burning. He realized suddenly that she was trying to get a head lock on him that he himself had taught her. He caught both her hands, twisting her right arm backward. She threw herself upon him violently, almost somersaulting over his shoulder, freeing her arm with a terrific jerk. Sven turned quickly, caught her about the waist with one arm and pressed the other against her throat, so that she was bent almost double and unable to breathe. He looked at her, saw that her eyes were closed and her face almost scarlet and dripping with perspiration.

"Had enough?" he asked, slightly loosening his hold.

Judith took advantage of the moment, and with a twist of her head was out of his grip like an eel. Her eyes were blazing, her breath coming in short gasps. She lashed out with her arm, striking him full across the face. While Sven, half stunned from the weight of the blow, was trying to understand the change in the issue, she hurled herself against him and he fell to the earth under her. Then something leaped in Sven. They were no longer unevenly matched, different in sex. They were two stark elements, striving for mastery over each other.

Sven crushed the girl's limbs between his own, bruised her throat, pulled her arms ruthlessly together behind her until the skin over the curve of her shoulders was white and taut, her clothing torn away. Her panting body heaved against his as they lay full length on the ground locked in furious embrace. Judith buried her nails in the flesh over his breast, beat her knees into his loins, set her teeth in the more tender skin over the veins at his wrists. She fought with insane abandon to any hurt he might inflict, or he would have mastered her at once. The faces, throats and chests of both were shining with sweat. Sven's breath fell in hot gusts on Judith's face. Suddenly her hand, that was fastened like steel on his throat, relaxed and fell away. Her eyelids quivered and a tear trickled down and mingled with the beads of perspiration on her temple. Sven released the arm that he had bent to breaking point. He was trembling.

"Judie," he muttered, "Judie—look at me."

Judith raised her eyelids slowly.

"Kiss me—now," she said in a breath.

than have him know, Caleb's children could wither and fall like rotten plants after frost—everything could fall into dissolution. He was his father's son, Mark Jordan, the son of the only man she had ever loved. Ellen, Martin, Judith and Charlie, they were only the offspring of Caleb Gare, they could be the sacrifice. She would bend and inure them to the land like implements, just as Caleb wished her to do. She would not intercede in their behalf hereafter. She would see them dry and fade into fruitlessness and grow old long before their time, but her heart would keep within itself and there would be no pity in her for the destruction of their youth. Amelia's face grew pale and hard as she knelt in the garden. A distinct change had come over her.

She carried the blanket indoors, thinking that it would be unnecessary to cover the tomatoes that night. The air seemed visible and intimate, as before rain. Her eyes wandered to the fields of tame hay and rye-grass that lay beyond the sheep pasture. There would be a tremendous yield this year. Always before, the sight of growth had somehow thrilled her, had struck a vital, creative chord within her that was otherwise left unsounded in this barren life. Now her mind was dulled by the sight of it. Growth—with death in its wake. She felt that in an instant her life had reached finality, that all the years behind her had been spent in a chrysalis, in a beginning. There had been no development in between—only a beginning and an end.

She went indoors and began energetically to polish the stove with a blackened cloth.

2

Before long Amelia returned to her old pale manner of self-effacement and submission, and the atmosphere on the Gare farm became normal once more to Lind's perception. The place was holding its breath again after a quiet exhalation.

Feeling that what had disturbed Amelia was at least for the present lulled, Lind approached her one day with a question. Mrs Gare was gathering eggs in the barn mangers, and, since it was Saturday morning, the Teacher had undertaken to help her.

"Mrs Gare, Mark Jordan would like very much to come here to see me, and to meet you people as well. Do you think Mr Gare would like to have him call?"

Amelia was prepared for just such a question. She smiled at Lind, and shook her head.

"I'm afraid it would only excite the children, Miss Archer, and stir up trouble. Mr Jordan would talk about things that we can't afford to think about."

"Well, then," said Lind, "will you permit Judie to come with me to see him? He is living there all alone and I think it would be kind to cook a good meal for him, now and then."

Amelia glanced at her, and looked away quickly.

"Judith might make an errand over that way, but don't speak of it before her father." Mark Jordan should have what he wanted, she resolved.

"I'll be careful not to, Mrs Gare," Lind said gratefully. She groped about in the hay and came upon another brown egg, which she placed carefully in the pan with the others. The feeling of conspiracy against Caleb was rather enjoyable.

She took the eggs to the house, and then went to the potato patch where Judith was absently hoeing between the rows. The sun was beating down upon the girl's bare head and on the strong honey-brown nape of her neck. A hot, dusty wind was stirring the tops of the dry potato plants. A little groove of dust had formed on either side of Judith's nose, and there were gray filaments of dust on the hair of her forearms. She crossed her arms and leaned forward on the hoe as Lind came up to her.

"A little romance, Judie," Lind said softly. "We're going to have supper to-morrow night with Mark Jordan —the man you saw me with at Yellow Post."

Judith frowned. To-morrow was Sunday. On Sundays Caleb usually went to the farm of one of the Icelanders in the afternoon, and did not return until late in the evening.

"Ma say I could go?"

Lind told her what Amelia had said. Judith was silent for a moment and then decided to confide in the Teacher to an extent.

"Will you let Sven come?"

"Why, that would be fine! We'll have a real party. If only Ellen and Martin could get away too. They never have any fun."

"No," said Jude with conviction. "They wouldn't enjoy themselves. Anyway, they mustn't know that Sven is going to be there—at least Ellen mustn't. Sven wants me to marry him, Lind, and go away to town."

Lind looked at her quietly for a moment. A change
had come over the girl during the past few days. She
was not so boisterous in her care of the animals, nor so
defiant toward the human beings on the farm as she had
been.

"And shall you?"

"Yes—before long. Don't let the others know."

Lind slipped away and Judith went on with her hoeing. She cast a resentful eye over the long rows of
potatoes. Food for another winter—another winter of
stumbling about in the bleak, icy dawn and tugging at
stubborn calves and hauling icicle-rimmed buckets full
of water through manure and frozen mud. Another
winter of inhibition and growing restiveness, and hope-
less dreaming of a better time to come. Another winter
under Caleb Gare . . . no, anything else was preferable.

As the work on the farm grew and grew, Judith was
struggling to see her way clear to liberty. Covertly she
watched Ellen and Amelia and Martin, even Charlie now
that he was learning to take his place, and saw them all
bowing without a question under the stupefying load.
And she recognized in herself an alien spirit, a violent
being of dark impulses, in no way related to the life about
her. She was alternately seized with an agony of pity
for Amelia, whose reticence she could not fathom, and
futile rage at Ellen and Martin for their endurance.
And beneath it all her passion for Sven pressed through
her being like an undercurrent of fire. She lay awake at
night with hot cheeks, thinking of him . . . of the day in
the clearing among the cedars . . . running her fingers
over the muscles of his throat. Caleb had not found out

that Lind had brought the cart home that day. She had not seen Sven since they had fought, had not wished to see him. She had need of an interim in which to think.

After another hour's work, Judith, looking up, saw Martin entering the gate from the pasture with three cows that were about to calve. More money for Caleb Gare, more toil for the workers under him. He had nearly twice as many cattle this year as three years ago: and no hired man now to help with their care, because Martin and Judith were old enough to do it together, and Judith strong enough to do it alone when Martin was otherwise occupied. In a hollow in the pasture she saw the sheep grazing, all of them shorn now, shorn of dollars and dollars worth of wool that would go toward the acquisition of more sheep . . . and more sheep . . . but not more freedom for the workers under Caleb Gare, not more joy in living. She remembered suddenly that the bag of wool she had got from her own sheep was still stowed away under the rafters in the loft. She must dispose of it some way before Caleb found it.

The hoe over her shoulder, Judith went to the barn where she found Martin, hammering new planks into the rotten floor.

"Martin," she began with difficulty. "Do you suppose he figures on getting a man for the haying?"

Martin looked at her dryly.

"Not with threshers askin' what they're goin' to. We'll be lucky if he hires a full crew. What you ask for?"

Judith threw herself down upon the threshold of the

barn door and leaned her head against the worn log frame. "Oh, nothing, but I was just thinkin' Ellen isn't really strong enough to help. Remember how she ran the fork into her foot last year 'cause she couldn't see it."

"Well—" Martin said slowly, "I'll ask him again."

Judith looked sideways at Martin where he was on his hands and knees fitting the new boards into the floor. She felt a sudden fullness of heart as she looked at him, and wished that somehow she might talk with him about things. She had always felt more kinship with Martin than with any of the others. How stooped already his shoulders were, how pitifully scrawny his neck! She watched him drive nails into the boards after he had fitted them, and saw how gentle his face was in the doing of the mean task. Why had she never seen these things in Martin before? Tears came into her eyes as they dwelt on him, and she could have rushed to him and thrown her arms about him from a sudden sheer realization of what he was. Martin would have been certain that she had gone out of her mind. She rose hastily and left him, before she should do the unaccountable thing.

Martin looked after her. In his uncertain way, he felt that it was not so much Ellen that Judith was concerned about. Jude was not adept at dissimulation.

His job in the barn done, Martin went to the pile of long, straight poplar logs he had cut, planed and measured for the new wagon shed. Martin was always building in his spare time. Caleb often chided him for the material and time he wasted on what he considered purely decorative and unnecessary outhouses, but since